No Woman Used Tony Manero. But Laura Was Something Else. . . .

The limousine was waiting outside the rehearsal studio, and suddenly Laura appeared, still in rehearsal clothes—tights and leg warmers over high-heeled sandals—but she'd thrown her fox fur over the costume and looked like a million before taxes.

"Tony."

"Yeah."

Her voice was surprisingly warm. "I'm having a few people over tonight. Sort of a pre-Christmas party type thing. Would you like to come?"

Tony stood eyeing her, hanging on desperately to his celebrated cool. "Didn't we have a big fight?" he wanted to know. "Wasn't that you?"

Laura smiled and shook her head. "Not quite. *We* didn't have a fight, *you* did."

He wanted to say no. With every nerve ending in his body, he willed himself to say no. "What time?" he asked.

"Ten."

Tony forced a shrug. "I don't know," was the best he could manage.

Laura nodded and stepped into the limo.

Wishing he could cut his tongue out, Tony asked, "Whose limo?" The car pulled away from the curb with a powerful surge of its noiseless engine. . . .

PARAMOUNT PICTURES PRESENTS
A ROBERT STIGWOOD PRODUCTION
A SYLVESTER STALLONE FILM
JOHN TRAVOLTA
"STAYING ALIVE"
Featuring Songs By THE BEE GEES
Executive Producer BILL OAKES
Based Upon Characters Created by NIK COHN
Written by SYLVESTER STALLONE and NORMAN WEXLER
Produced by ROBERT STIGWOOD and SYLVESTER STALLONE
Directed by SYLVESTER STALLONE
A PARAMOUNT PICTURE

STAYING ALIVE

A novel by Leonore Fleischer
from the screenplay
written by Sylvester Stallone
and Norman Wexler
based upon characters
created by Nik Cohn

PUBLISHED BY POCKET BOOKS NEW YORK

Another *Original* publication of POCKET BOOKS

POCKET BOOKS, a division of Simon & Schuster, Inc.
1230 Avenue of the Americas, New York, N.Y. 10020

ISBN: 0-671-49690-5

First Special printing July, 1983

10 9 8 7 6 5 4 3 2 1

To all the fancy dancers

STAYING ALIVE

CHORUS CALL

NON-EQ., Morecombe Theater, HI-STEPPIN' 12/21 at 10 A.M. and 2 P.M. at the theater, Broome and Prince Sts. in Soho. A non-Equity chorus call will be held for Eq. candidates for a new off-Broadway musical for the fall of 1983. Dancers who can sing and look good (tall preferred) are asked to come prepared to do it all. Producer, Herbert Weinstein, Choreographer, Paul Diamante, Director to be announced.

Mon. 12/21—non-Equity male dancers
10 A.M.–12 noon.
Mon. 12/21–non-Equity female dancers
2 P.M.–4 P.M.

Chapter One

TONY MANERO MADE SURE TO GET THERE
*extra early. Even so there were more than three dozen
kids there ahead of him, and when his turn came up on
the line, he was handed the number forty, scrawled in
black marker on a piece of white paperboard with a
pin attached.*

*There was no place for them to get ready except
behind the back wall of the stage, and there the boys
were peeling down to their dance tights, shucking off
their jeans and shirts quickly and professionally.
Those who were already in dance clothes were doing
warm-ups, limbering up with bends and extensions,
filling their lungs with long deep breaths.*

*He dropped his gym bag on the floor in front of the
wall between a redhead who sat immobile in the lotus
position, concentrating on his mantra to center himself, and a long-haired blond boy he recognized
vaguely from other auditions. They nodded to each
other warily, competitors.*

*He took his denim jacket off and folded it neatly,
dropped it to the dusty floor and placed his pants on
top of it. He was already wearing a dance belt and*

*black tights and a skintight T-shirt of a flexible jersey
that moved with him without hampering him. From his
bag he took a black sweatband, which he pulled down
over his brow, and a pair of leg warmers. Then he
changed into his dance shoes and looked around him.*

*The place was filling up. Perhaps two hundred pro-
fessional dancers and would-be professional dancers
were here already, lured by the call in the trade
papers. Every one of them was determined to make it,
desperate to be chosen. This wasn't even Broadway;
this was off-Broadway; even so it was what they were
living for.*

The crewcut dude in the tinfoil jumpsuit who took a
walk on the moon proclaiming "one small step for
man, one giant leap for mankind," didn't know anything. If you want to take a giant leap, try crossing the
bridge from Brooklyn to Manhattan. Two different
worlds, my friend, more different even than earth and
moon.

Four years ago Tony Manero took that leap and
crossed that East River bridge. He left behind his own
world in Bay Ridge, Brooklyn, a world where he was
undisputed king of the mountain. The best dancer, the
sharpest dresser, the baddest cat with the chicks; in
Bay Ridge, Tony was a Somebody. But Bay Ridge was
a very puny mountain to be king of, and Tony had got
itchy. Out there somewhere over the bridge lay the
larger world, shimmering with glamour and excitement, pulsating with hot music and sensational
women, and it was waiting for Tony Manero.

Wrong. Once he crossed that bridge, Tony discovered that Manhattan waited for nobody. It moved on,
cold and mean to all but a handful of the lucky ones.
Without the breaks even those who had been Some-
bodies in Bay Ridge found themselves Nobodies in
Manhattan.

Instead of glamour and excitement Tony discovered
hard work and rejection. Instead of glittering nights

there were cold gray mornings in winter, steamy, muggy mornings in summer and a lot of hard luck in between. Breaking into the theater is only slightly less difficult than performing open-heart surgery when you've never been to medical school, but Tony was prepared for that. What he wasn't prepared for was how much the constant rejection could hurt, how much it cost to live in even the rattiest fleabag single room in Manhattan, how hard it would be to find an everyday paying job. In Bay Ridge he'd had everything knocked. His mother dished up the pasta and the sauce and urged him to eat; his own room was his private sanctum; his friends were always available to run his errands and take his orders. And every Saturday night he bestrode the narrow world of the Odyssey Disco like a dancing colossus. Tony Manero, the guy every girl in Brooklyn wanted to dance with, the guy almost all of them wanted to be with. In Manhattan that first year he'd been forced to wash dishes or load dresses on a wheeled rack to push through the overcrowded streets of the garment district. Instead of his mother's nourishing meals, he'd grabbed fast-food cheeseburgers and greasy fries. And that was on his good days; most of the time hunger kept his belly growling like an angry alley cat.

But he went hungry almost gladly to pay for the head shots, the dance classes, the roof over his head, an occasional something to wear. Gone were the days when Tony always had a new shirt or a pair of two-tone shoes with Cuban heels put by on layaway to be picked up on payday. Compared with four years ago, he was practically ragged. But he didn't mind that either. He didn't mind the cold or the heat or living in tap city the way he had to just to get by. Because despite all the frustrations and the setbacks, despite all the rejections and the failed auditions, Tony's dream was still alive, still burning.

He would make it. Of all the thousands of hopefuls who flock hungrily to New York every year to make it in the theater—of all the thousands of actors, dancers, singers who join the thousands of actors, dancers, singers already in New York banging on the doors, only the smallest handful ever make it at all, let alone big. But Tony was determined even after all this time to be among that handful who rise to the top and shine among the stars.

Where this conviction, deep and purposeful, kept welling up from, he couldn't say. But it was there, it was real, and it kept him going. Someday he'd be known, he'd be big, not only in Bay Ridge, but in Manhattan. And Manhattan was the world. When Tony made it to the top, doors would open and famous faces would smile at him; celebrated hands would be held out for him to shake. He'd be one of them, warm and well fed, admired, loved, respected and secure. Of this he was certain.

Tony pinned his number on his shirt. It was almost time for them to begin. A small sarcastic man with a scarf tied around his neck and another around his waist, Fred Astaire style, was bustling around with a clipboard, explaining fussily that they would be auditioned twenty at a time.

"That means that those of you wearing numbers one through twenty will be on first, and those of you wearing numbers twenty-one through forty will go on second, forty-one through sixty will be next, and so forth. Have you all got that?"

"What does he think we are, morons?" muttered Tony to the boy standing next to him, receiving an indifferent shrug in response. They always treated you like you were dumb; dancers were said to have their brains in their feet.

He'd be auditioning with the second group. Good. It would give him a chance to study both the competition and the routine.

Around him the stage was alive with the noise of

dancers' feet and voices as anxiety rose to fever pitch in the last few minutes before the audition would begin. It wasn't possible to remain cool; Tony found that the palms of his hands were icy cold and clammy with chilled sweat. There was an economic recession going full blast out there in the real world, and fewer shows were being brought to Broadway. Fewer still to off-Broadway. This meant, of course, fewer jobs for actors and dancers. How many dancers were they looking to cast for this show? Twelve, maybe four-teen—girls and boys together. And there were over two hundred hopefuls milling around on this stage, each of them at least good, some very good, and all desperate to be chosen.

Four years ago when he'd crossed over that bridge, what did he have going for him? At nineteen he boasted a good physique, tall with big shoulders. Thick black hair, soft and wavy, that his groupies had begged to be allowed to touch. Large eyes of a surprising blue, two unexpected sapphires in a dark Italian face. A cleft chin, long legs, a one-way grin.

And he could dance. He'd been the emperor of the disco. When Tony took the floor, everybody stood back and watched. Tony Manero had the moves. He pranced and strutted and jerked his hips. His eyes flashed; his gestures commanded. He was disco itself, Saturday night come to life. The girls lapped it up, and even the other guys had to applaud him grudgingly. How could they help it? Tony Manero was the best. Everybody in Bay Ridge knew it.

Dancing seemed to be the only way out of Bay Ridge, the key to the door that held Tony a prisoner. Dancing was what set him apart from everybody around him, gave him his edge. Dancing was what made Tony happy. When he moved to music, it was better than talking; he could make his meaning plain to everybody who saw him. Flaunting his masculinity like a rooster in a henyard. It was, in essence, everything that held meaning in his life. It *was* his life.

So he made his mind up. He'd dance. It was what he liked best, what he *did* best. He'd dance his way to fame and fortune in the New York theater. Which is why he crossed the bridge.

And the first thing Tony found out was that he didn't know how to dance. Maybe for Saturday night, but not for the theater. Disco was one thing, but the complex, stylized and artfully choreographed athletic ballets required of show dancers were totally foreign to Tony. He'd never had the right training, in fact he'd never had any dance training at all. His muscles were wrong, neither long enough nor developed enough for a dancer. Even the body he was so proud of wasn't right. It was ten pounds overweight by the standards of a professional dancer. A dancer's body is as finely tuned and sharply honed as a precision instrument, as trim and sleek as a perfectly designed airfoil. One is never aware of flesh on a dancer, only of bone and sinew.

Tony Manero thought that all he'd have to do was show them his moves, and they'd be all over him. What a comedown! His first audition was a disaster.

He'd bought a copy of *Back Stage* and circled all the open auditions for chorus dancers. He was willing to start small. Fourteen dancers were being cast, seven men and seven women, and two hundred and sixty-seven kids showed up to audition. They were seen forty at a time for the purposes of early elimination, and Tony was among the first to be cut.

He was stunned. Incredulous. It wasn't a complicated routine they were asked to perform, but it was a demanding one, and Tony's body just couldn't make the moves. It looked so easy and graceful, but that was deceptive. All around him boys and girls were leaping, spinning, kicking and bending, and Tony was nailed to the floor with a pain in the small of his back and a right hamstring that was screaming bloody murder. In the

three minutes of the preliminary audition, Tony felt
dumber and more helpless than he'd felt since he was a
little kid taking a belting from his old man.

He limped gratefully off the stage with the other
rejects, his heart somewhere in the pit of his belly. It
seemed to him in the black moments of his humiliation
that his dream had shattered and the fragments of it
were sticking in his throat, choking him. Because it
couldn't be tears; men didn't cry. He'd left Bay Ridge
with such high hopes and such grandiose expectations
that he'd shared with anybody who would listen; how
the hell could he slink back home with his tail shivering between his legs?

But later that night on the thin lumpy mattress that
dared to call itself a bed, as every muscle in Tony's
overweight body jumped in agonized protest, the
dream began to put itself together again in spite of it
all. He could dance, he knew he could! There were
two differences between him and the group who'd
been chosen to audition a second time. The first difference was that they knew a whole different set of
moves from his. The second difference was that once
he'd learned those moves, he'd be better than any one
of them. It wasn't a defeat. It was a challenge.

The next morning Tony set to work. He found a job
in a Lincoln Center restaurant washing dishes. It
didn't pay much, and the hours were long, but they
were staggered, with enough free time during the day
for Tony to take care of other business. He went to
another audition, and this time he kept his eyes open.
He flunked of course, within the first couple of minutes, but now he could see a little more clearly what he
was doing wrong. He waited backstage, and when
one of the dancers who was chosen came out, he
stopped him, asked him how he'd learned to dance so
well.

The young man's eyebrows shot up toward his
hairline, but he made a courteous reply and gave Tony
the name and address of a good dance teacher, Duke

Miller. With the precious piece of paper safely stowed in his pocket, Tony embarked on his new life.

The choreographer was now walking out on stage, and a silence fell among the young dancers. This was serious business, no more time for gossip and exchanging phone numbers. His fussy little assistant in the scarves rapped his pencil on his clipboard for attention.

"All right, everybody! Clear the stage, please, except for the first twenty. And please have your résumés ready in case you're asked to come back. Just numbers one through twenty, and hurry, people, we haven't all day."

Tony was among the last to leave the stage so that he could stand in the front rank of the crowded wings and watch the choreographer explain and demonstrate the routine he was auditioning.

Out in the empty theater in row G center section, sat the producer and the director, tired and somewhat bored. The floor around them was littered with empty coffee containers made of Styrofoam and discarded pink paper envelopes that once held calorie-free artificial sweetener. A couple of gofers, also armed with clipboards and anxious expressions, hovered on the fringes of the aisle, waiting for orders.

Up on the stage the choreographer, a very thin man with a close-cropped head and tightly shaped beard and mustache to match, had finished demonstrating the routine and was standing with his hands on his nonexistent hips, waiting for the music to begin. They only showed you twice or at the most three times; if you couldn't pick up a dance routine after seeing it twice, they didn't want you in their show.

It was a simple routine to learn, but a tricky one to execute, requiring coordination, balance and grace. Definitely one that would separate the men from the boys. But he could do it, he could definitely do it, thought Tony as the piano player broke into the open-

ing chords, and music poured out. On the stage twenty
bodies swung into immediate action; twenty limber
knees came hurtling up to twenty skinny chests; forty
arms were flung wide.

Hey, I know that guy, thought Tony in sudden dis-
may, taking a longer look at the choreographer. He
saw a thin-lipped man in a beautifully cut silk shirt
tucked into pleated flannel trousers, immaculate and
critical. Didn't I audition for him before? Hell, this
time he's not gonna turn me down!

This time I'm gonna make it!

The dance teacher had been dubious, because Tony
Manero was really too old to begin training; most
dancers are dancing by the age of ten. But something
in the kid's face—the determination darkening his
eyes to navy blue, the stubborn set of his lips and
chin—made Duke Miller hesitate, then finally accept
Tony as his pupil, even though it was a shame to take
the kid's money.

But Duke Miller wound up earning every penny he
charged. Tony's energy was ferocious, and he sopped
up instruction like a dry sponge. He practiced with
such enthusiasm and zeal, despite the pain in his
lengthening muscles, that he was out of beginners'
class and into intermediate by the end of the seventh
week. It took some hard pounding to get Tony out of
the staccato rhythms of disco movement and into the
smooth flow of jazz dancing, which is partly based on
classical ballet and partly on the innovations of modern dance, but it began to happen for him.

Tony had never heard of Martha Graham, he'd
never seen a ballet in his life, and he'd never disciplined himself before, but he learned quickly. As ten
pounds dropped from his frame, and new muscle
groups began to develop, it started to *feel* right. Once
again he began to take joy in the music, and when he
improvised, it was with a surer understanding of his

body's relationship to the space around it and with a commanding grace he'd never before possessed.

He began to go to auditions again, and although he was still eliminated every time, once or twice he made the second cut, the ones who were called back for another try. As his skill increased, his confidence grew. He started to understand that the language of dance that he used to speak with his body was like a baby's first words compared to the fluency he was developing. His body language was often a shout of triumph now.

But he had yet to be cast in a show. Whatever it was that held him back, he had not passed a single audition, although choreographers often regarded him thoughtfully as he moved, almost tempted to give him a try. Because he had talent, that much was obvious. It was raw, it was surrounded by rough edges like a diamond waiting to be cut and polished into full brilliance, but it *was* talent. Yet each time a choreographer or a director or a producer was tempted by the panther grace of Tony Manero, he or she had second thoughts. Putting on a Broadway show had problems enough of its own without taking on a diamond in the rough. Hell with it.

The routine was drawing to a close, and the first group was almost finished. When the music ended, the dancers broke out of formation like a flock of startled birds, their sweaty faces expressing their nervousness. The choreographer was eyeing them rather grimly, his thin lips pursed.

"Numbers two . . . seven . . . eight and eleven stay backstage. The rest can go. Thank you."

Four faces lit up with happiness, and sixteen sets of shoulders drooped in disappointment. The choreographer turned toward the wings where Tony was standing.

"Next lineup!" he barked. "Let's go. Look alive!"

There was a rustle out in the empty audience as the

*producer summoned an eager gofer to his side and
whispered into his ear. As the second group of dancers
came out on the stage, the gofer was rushing up to the
apron.*

"Just a minute!" he called.

*Frowning, the choreographer turned. "What is it?"
he demanded impatiently.*

"Forget number eleven."

"Why? He moves well!"

"The producer doesn't like his face."

*The choreographer's eyes rolled up in a grimace of
exasperation, but he said nothing. After all, his job
was on the line, and he wasn't about to risk it for one
dancer out of a thousand, not for a chorus boy.*

*"Number eleven, a mistake has been made," he
called. "You're not right."*

*The elation died on the dancer's face and he turned,
stricken.*

*"Did I do something wrong?" he faltered, unable to
believe his bad luck. His face was red with the humiliation of being rejected in front of his colleagues.*

"Your back extension is too stiff. Work on it."

*Thoroughly crushed, the dancer slunk off the stage,
and the choreographer turned his crisp, somewhat
sour attention to the second group as they took their
places according to the numbers on their shirts.*

*"If you are all professionals, by now the routine
should be committed to memory, so let's do it! Music!"*

As time passed, and Tony's dancing improved, so
did some other parts of his life. He wasn't washing
dishes anymore. Instead he'd lucked into a job busing
tables and tending bar at a dancing club called The
Savage Instinct. It was hard work, and the decibel
level was deafening, but Tony enjoyed the pulsating
vitality, and the tips were often good.

But, jeez, life in New York City was expensive!
Here he was living in the cruddiest one-room-occu-

pancy apartment hotel on the seediest block in the
Upper West Side, but his one crummy room cost him
eighty-five a week. Even McDonald's food cost three
or four bucks a throw, especially the way Tony could
put it away. He remembered with an ache in his gut the
way his mother would stand at the stove, one hand
filled with raw pasta, poised to fling the spaghetti into
the boiling water the minute the door was opened and
her husband or one of her sons walked through it. At
least in Bay Ridge he had eaten well—veal with pep-
pers, chicken cacciatore, minestrone and fried cala-
mari; Tony could drool just remembering the table his
mother would set. Even though her lasagna had been
so heavy it lay on your stomach for a week reminding
you of its presence, Tony was often so hungry he felt
he could kill for a leaden plateful of it.

*As the music rolled off the piano keys in an up,
bright tempo, Tony and nineteen other young hopefuls
began to dance.*

*Nineteen bodies moved professionally, smoothly
through the routine, kicking, turning, gliding. Across
nineteen faces were spread wide, bright, professional
smiles. Only one face didn't smile, only one body
danced not to the music, but from it, the movements
coming out of the heart of the beat. To even the most
ignorant observer, Tony Manero was different from
the others.*

*As the music built and the tempo quickened, Tony
grew even more concentrated, more focused in the
dance. It appeared to possess him, to take him over, to
move his body interpretively in subtle, complex ways.
He moved differently from the others; where they were
mechanical, he was real—living, intense, almost ani-
malistic.*

*The routine was drawing to a rapid close, and the
dancers threw themselves into the prescribed crouch,*

their arms flung behind them. Only Tony's arms
reached for the stars—a wide, exuberant gesture.

"Wait! What the hell are you doing? What the hell
are you doing?!" roared the choreographer angrily.

The dancers came to a nervous standstill as nine-
teen of them looked fearfully at the neat little man with
the angry face. Only Tony Manero remained in a kind
of trance, locked tightly within himself.

"You, I'm talking to you!" the choreographer
barked, glaring at Tony.

At an audition one day he met a girl named Jackie
Call—small, blond, pretty rather than beautiful, but
with a sweetness about her that cut through the bull-
shit that usually separated Tony from the women he
went out with. Jackie came from Omaha and laughed
when she learned that Tony thought Omaha was somewhere out west like Wyoming or Utah. They seemed
to come from different planets, but like two planets in
a magnetic field, they were drawn toward each other.

Jackie was a professional dancer who actually
worked now and then. She'd been in three shows since
she'd come to New York six years before, and one of
them had become a hit and had provided her with
steady work for seventeen months. Most of the time
however, she supported herself by teaching advanced
dance classes at Fatima's Dance Land. By the time
one of the male instructors there quit his job, she and
Tony were, as they say, an item. So she brought Tony
to meet Fatima, and he took on a second job, teaching
jazz dancing to dance illiterates. The bread came in
very handy, especially when he and Jackie moved in
together.

Their relationship was a puzzle to Jackie. Never in
her life had she met anyone like Tony Manero; he was
an enigma to her. As intimate as they were, sharing the
same small apartment, she knew almost nothing about
him. He never talked about his family or about Bay

Ridge. He never once spoke tenderly to her or asked her about her feelings. The word *feelings* never even passed his lips. He made it plain that he enjoyed her, but it seemed to her to go no further than that. She was a pleasant presence to him, a good dance partner and not much more.

What did he talk about? Dancing. Getting that first break, the big one. Getting to the top. He appeared obsessed with his career, almost to the exclusion of everything else. Jackie was more laid back; she enjoyed music, books, paintings. She wanted to go to museums with Tony, to concerts and plays and Shakespeare in the Park and all the enjoyments that New York offers. She even wanted to go with Tony to Bay Ridge to meet his parents when Tony made one of his rare trips home. Not for the conventional reasons, but to get to know a little better the man she was living with.

But Tony said no to everything, and eventually it got to Jackie's head.

So the frustration led to bickering, and the bickering to fighting, and one night Tony went home to the fleabag West Side hotel where he still lived.

They remained friends though; since both of them continued to work at Fatima's Dance Land, it seemed the only civilized thing to do. Also they genuinely liked each other, if not something more. But *what* more, Jackie was never able to figure out, and Tony never gave her any help.

"Wait! What the hell are you doing? What the hell are you doing?! You! I'm talking to you!"

Tony came slowly out of his trance, realizing that the choreographer was yelling directly at him. The music had stopped and the other nineteen dancers were giving him the hairy eyeball, relief mingled with disdain.

"Who told you to raise your arms like that?" the choreographer demanded through tight lips.

Tony shrugged innocently. "Nobody."

"Well, why did you do it?"

Tony's brows contracted in a frown. This turkey was beginning to get to him. "I'm just doing what I feel," he answered, keeping his anger under control.

"You're supposed to be doing what I feel!" snapped the smaller man. "You're not auditioning for some disco free-for-all." His words dripped contempt. "Grandstanding throws everybody else's timing off, or don't you care?"

Stung by the sarcasm, Tony looked around him. The other dancers, delighted to eliminate at least one of the competition, stared at him either blankly or with dislike. It was obvious that they were on the choreographer's side, ranged against Tony.

A muscle jumped in Tony's lean jaw, and his eyes darkened to the blue of the ocean depths. "I said I just do what I feel," he explained again. It was not an apology.

The choreographer's eyes narrowed, and his head gave a crisp little nod. "I know you do. I have seen you at auditions five times. So by now I hope you know you don't have it, so don't waste my time again. Try American Bandstand."

Having delivered himself of this crushing opinion, the choreographer turned to the piano player and raised his hand. "Once again."

Tony's face was flushed with rage, and his eyes glittered like two blue diamonds. You don't have it! Who was this creep to tell Tony Manero he didn't have it? He took a step forward.

"Hey," he called in a hard voice.

"Five, six, seven, eight . . ." The choreographer ignored him, counting off for the other dancers.

But Tony took a step forward, all six foot two of him, heavily muscled, fists clenched, and the smaller man took an instinctive step backward.

"What do you want?" His voice held enough fear almost to quaver, but not quite.

"You don't know me good enough to tell me what I am," said Tony angrily. Then he began to stalk off the stage.

At the sight of his back, the choreographer found the courage to call after him. *"I may not know you, but I know dance, which is more than I can say for you. All right, once again. Take it from the third turn. . . ."*

Disgusted and hurt, Tony started for the wings, but at the last moment, a thought struck him, and he came back out on the stage, peering down into the empty orchestra until he saw the producer sitting in Row G.

"Wait," called Tony loudly, and the piano stopped. *"I gotta say something about this here or I won't be able to digest tonight."* He glared down at the producers' group, his fists on his hips, as dangerous as a young jungle cat. *"Y'know, I might not be the best dancer in the world, but this guy here wouldn't know a good performer if Fred Astaire was to tap dance on his lips!"*

From behind him he heard gasps and then giggles as the dancers were dumbstruck. He could hear the choreographer's breath being let out in an angry hiss like a cat whose tail had been stepped on, and the mincing little assistant gave an explosive *"Well!"*

Tony spread his hands out, palms facing the orchestra. *"That's it. I'm done now,"* he said mildly and loped off on the balls of his feet, exhilarated at having spoken his piece. Maybe he should have done that months ago.

But as he collected his things and slipped on his pants, jacket and street shoes, his exhilaration began to wane. Defeat crept silently into his bones, drawing down the corners of his mouth and making his face look suddenly older and more tired.

Listlessly and in silence he left the theater, barely

aware that the dancers still waiting to go on were staring after him curiously. One more audition shot to hell.

Outside it had grown considerably colder. Out on the street he shivered and headed uptown. He still had to go to work.

Chapter Two

GETTING OUT OF THE SUBWAY AT EIGHTY-sixth Street, Tony walked a few blocks south. Broadway uptown really looks crummy in daylight—newspapers and other garbage being blown around the streets, junkies and winos in every second doorway. But there's a vigor to it, a mix of old people and young, of welfare mothers and middle-class families from West End Avenue and the Drive shopping in the same Korean fruit markets and taking their dry cleaning to the same laundromat. Blacks, whites, Hispanics, mongrel dogs on leashes, supermarkets and frozen yogurt parlors, seedy movie theaters showing arty foreign films and revivals of Ruby Keeler musicals, Szechuan restaurants, soup-and-salad joints with imitation sidewalk cafés—all of these tickled Tony most of the time, and he usually bopped down upper Broadway with a grin on his face.

Not today though. Today his shoulders drooped under the weight of depression. The anger, swift and cleansing, had worn off and had left in its wake a feeling of hopelessness. Why was he working his tail off when every two-bit choreographer held the upper hand and could order him off the stage? He felt as if he were in a long, long tunnel with no daylight showing and not the smallest hint of when he'd see any.

At Eighty-third Street he crossed over to the east side of Broadway and entered a narrow doorway with a sign reading

FATIMA'S DANCE LAND

Ballet   Tap   Aerobics   Jazz

Expert Instruction
Reasonable Fees
Second Floor

These days dance is probably the most popular of the art forms next to film, and more people are getting into it. Dance studios have cropped up all over New York, many of them in classy, expensive locations. Check this out. A large comfortable studio reached by elevators with Muzak. Perfect stretches of hardwood floor gleaming and professional. Indirect lighting and unbroken expanses of mirror. Locker rooms with lockers that really lock, dressing rooms with piped-in music. Showers, sauna, Jacuzzi, even masseurs. Flowers in the reception area. A little fridge filled with Perrier bottled water. Spacious private studios for each teacher and small classes—of no more than eight or ten—so that each student gets individual instruction. Got the picture? Good.

Now throw it away and try to conjure up its exact opposite and you'll have Fatima's Dance Land.

First there were no elevators, and if there were, you could bet they wouldn't be working. Tony ran up a long dark flight of stairs covered in ancient and cracked linoleum. The stairway was so narrow that the walls were permanently rubbed dark at shoulder height and hadn't been painted since the building was put up more than fifty years ago.

Next the reception area, if you could call it that, was a cubicle about ten by thirteen feet with a rickety, decrepit desk in the center behind which Fatima sat. The ceiling had never been painted, and the room itself was rarely dusted above table level. Flowers were there, but they were plastic, a sprig of artificial roses stuck into the dusty soil of a pothos plant that was struggling not to die and losing the fight. Against one wall stood a vending machine that dispensed, if you were lucky, Sprite, Tab and Coca Cola and revolting little cheese crackers filled with gluey peanut butter. Everything cost sixty-five cents, and the machine didn't make change but would swallow three quarters with greedy glee and give you back *bupkiss*.

This reception area, tiny as it was, was usually crammed with students, and today was no exception. About eight or nine women and four men were occupying the two or three battered chairs, standing against the dingy walls and even sitting on the floor, waiting for Tony's class to begin. Some of them had just completed an earlier class and were still sweating, rubbing at their hair with their own towels; there were no showers at Fatima's, and the dressing rooms were so miniscule that they were tacitly reserved for the instructors.

The sound of chattering voices, most of them female, assaulted Tony's ears as he pushed open the studio door. Weight and diet, clothing, auditions, chiropractors, aches and pains, unfaithful boyfriends—all these were common topics to be exchanged freely and at the tops of the dancers' lungs.

In the center of all this babel sat Fatima, paying no attention as usual, selling dance tickets and punching cards like a train conductor. She was a tall handsome black woman, unflappable and street smart, who had danced with the Alvin Ailey company until a bad knee forced her off the stage. About five years ago she had sunk every penny she'd saved into this seedy dance studio on the Upper West Side, and she guarded her investment like a dragon guards his gold, breathing fire. As Tony came in, Fatima threw him a sour look.

"C'mon, c'mon," she called to him with an impatient shake of her head that sent her long earrings dancing against her cheek. "The class is full, and you're late! Why are you late?"

Tony gave her a wry little smile, tinged with bitterness. "My Rolls got towed."

Fatima clicked her tongue against her teeth. "No jokes. We got people here—" She waved a long, dark hand in the direction of the mob scene.

"I had this audition," Tony said quietly. He walked past her on his way to the dressing room, and the dejection in his face and body caught her attention at last.

"No excuses," she told him, but her voice was a trifle less stern.

Tony's little smile widened to a grin. "If I gave you a million dollars, would ya not be mad?" he asked impishly.

Fatima shook her head in mock exasperation. "Yeah," she allowed, trying to keep her voice gruff.

Digging his hand into his pants pocket, Tony came up with a coin. "All right. Here's twenty-five cents on account." He spun the quarter at her, and Fatima captured it expertly, rewarding him with a smile.

He felt better. The old charm was still going for him. He was, after all, totally irresistible.

The dozen students from the outer office were waiting for him in his studio when he came out in his tights and dance shoes. His studio. It was to laugh. Each of the studios was in continual use; Fatima should have revolving doors installed. A professional dance class employed a piano, and a jazz class sometimes even had a drummer too, but Fatima's teachers relied on tape players which had to be started, stopped, rewound constantly. Still it was just as well. The dance instructor usually had to pay for the accompanist out of his or her own money, and what Fatima paid Tony would not keep a hamster alive.

He got ten dollars for every hour he taught plus three dollars a head for every student in his class. For this hour for example he'd make thirty-six dollars. Not a bad hourly rate, but not a lot if you worked only one hour a week. Tony had to work at least one other job simultaneously, which made for a helluva lot of running his behind off, not to mention keeping strange hours.

The students—many of whom were novices, a handful would-be professionals, with overweight housewives mixed into the group—paid six dollars for a class, but could buy a dance card good for ten classes for fifty dollars. This allowed them to come and go pretty much as they pleased, taking classes when their mood was right or when they had the time. So Tony never was sure how much money he'd be earning; it could range from a low of about twenty-two dollars up to seventy dollars an hour, when Fatima crammed a class with more students than it should really hold.

Even so he was a popular instructor. His flashing good looks, his general air of enthusiasm and the despotic way he ran his class contributed to his popularity. But what really kept his students faithful and coming back for more was the way Tony moved, the sheer power and poetry of his dancing. Maybe if they hung around long enough, some of Tony's talent might rub off on them.

The stifling heat in the studio and the smell of the room hit Tony in the face like a stale flounder. Dancers never dance in air conditioning; the muscles must be kept warm, so studios are usually kept at high temperatures. In the winter steam hisses out of large radiators; in the summer the heat from the streets rises and floats in through the opened windows, bringing with it the noises of city traffic, police sirens wailing, dogs barking—New York City in full cry. Mingled with the heat are always the odors—sweat, rosin, dirty dance clothes and even what the students have eaten for lunch or dinner. It was an atmosphere you could cut with a dull-bladed knife, but to Tony it was sweet perfume. It was part of dance.

The walls of his studio had recently been painted with a cheap bright paint that was already peeling off in garish strips as though the room had been flayed. But no amount of paint could disguise the fact that the floor was badly worn and filled with rough spots, soft as cheese. Also the mirror along the wall was not one large clear expanse of glass, but a series of murky ones hung at different times and reflecting slightly distorted images with large seams down the middle where the panes joined. As the students lined up, they jostled each other for the best positions in front of the glass.

Tony was in total control; this was his domain, and he was the king of it.

Quickly and skillfully he led them through a warm-up at the barre, then illustrated a combination for them, dancing with style and arrogance to the brash music from the tape player. He showed them once, twice, a third time.

"Okay, your turn. Let's go."

Leading them in the routine, he kept his eyes on the glass, checking his students out. Some of his class danced with more skill than the rest, the result of more practice, but none of them had much confidence or any real style.

"Eyes on the mirror . . . watch yourself . . . watch your line . . . your back. Float! That's the feeling you want to get . . . arms extended . . . good, good . . . keep the energy up."

For most of them, floating was an uphill struggle.

"Put it all together. Attitude! A lot of attitude! You're strong . . . you're proud . . . ya got attitude. . . ."

Twelve mediocre-to-bad dancers tried to present a picture of strong and proud. Pretty hopeless.

Tony turned from the mirror to look at his little class, and there was a shadow of pity in his blue eyes.

"I think we've got some real attitude in this group," he told them without conviction, smiling weakly. The depression was coming back now, heavy with gloom, and the remainder of the class hour dragged by slowly.

Tony had just finished putting on his street clothes in the stuffy little closet that passed for a men's dressing room and was stuffing his dance gear into his vinyl gym bag when he heard a knock at the door.

"Tony!" a voice called. Jackie's voice.

"Yeah."

"What happened?"

"About what?" Tony called back, pretending not to understand, although he knew very well what Jackie was asking.

"About what? About how you did at the audition."

Pulling the zipper up on his bag almost savagely, Tony stepped out of the dressing room. Jackie was standing in the hallway, a look of concern on her pretty features, her green eyes slightly worried under the golden wings of her brows.

"So what happened?" she demanded again.

Tony shrugged. "I turned 'em down."

Jackie bit her lip, disturbed by the cloud over Tony's face and by the hurt apparent in his eyes. She walked beside him as he made his way toward the front door; it was hard keeping pace with Tony, even though her own legs were long for her height.

"Really, what happened?" she begged.

Tony didn't bother to look at her; he couldn't meet her eyes. "They didn't like my moves," he threw over his shoulder.

Jackie put one hand on his arm, slowing him down.

"They don't know anything, so don't let it get you down," she murmured sympathetically.

He turned to look at her, seeing a slender girl with a short cap of blond hair and the pixie face of a gamine. He could see real caring on that face, real concern for him, and it both touched him and made him feel a little uncomfortable. But he was used to feeling that way around Jackie, ambivalent.

"I never felt this good," he lied, not even bothering to disguise his depression. Then, "Ow!" he yelled, pulling his arm away from her. Jackie had seized it and sunk her teeth into it.

"Hey! What? You skip lunch or something?" He rubbed at his arm. It still stung where Jackie's sharp little white teeth had nipped it smartly.

"Getting your mind off that audition." Jackie grinned.

Tony couldn't help grinning back; Jackie's smile was not to be resisted. "So now I gotta worry about rabies."

Jackie gave a flip little toss of her head and turned down the corridor.

"Listen, can ya wait a minute?" Tony called after her.

But Jackie didn't stop. "I have to get going," she yelled back.

Tony started after her. "One minute!" he wheedled. "C'mon."

The girl shook her golden head. "I have to shower and get to the theater. I can't be late."

"Forget the shower, you look immaculate," joked Tony. "C'mon, Jackie." He had caught up with her now and had placed a restraining hand on her arm. "Be mature for a minute and wait here. I'd wait for you."

Jackie looked up into his face, feeling a familiar tug at her insides at the sight of his big blue eyes and persuasive smile. He could still get to her, even after a year or more apart. ". . . Sure you would," she told him sarcastically, but both of them knew she'd wait.

He loped off to the reception area, where he found Fatima entering the day's receipts into a well-thumbed ledger.

"Fatima, got a second? Hey, you look great tonight," he told her all in one breath. "That dress is a good color for you. We once had a car that color, very nice."

Fatima barely looked up from her writing, paying no attention at all to Tony's breathless patter.

"What do you need?" she asked, her eyes still on the column of figures. She was a woman of few words.

Tony bit his lip and plunged in. "Well, what I got on my mind is teachin' a second class."

"No."

"What I'm sayin' is I got all these other aggravatin' part-time jobs, so I spend all my life runnin' back and forth, back and forth . . ."

"Slow down," Fatima advised laconically.

"Say what?" Tony looked blank.

"Slow down. You'll live longer."

Tony watched her for a beat, waiting for her to say something else. But not another word was forthcoming. "No" appeared to be Fatima's final word on the subject.

"Thanks, Fatima," Tony said sarcastically. "This talk has done me a lot of good." Then when there was still no reply, Tony stalked out of her office, fuming. Jackie was waiting for him in the corridor, as he'd known she would be.

"How'd it go?" she asked him for the second time that day.

Tony shook his head glumly. "No extra class."

Jackie smiled up at him. "Don't worry about it," she said consolingly. "She'll give you another class. The customers really like you."

"Yeah," answered Tony in a hollow voice. "I'm a regular cult figure. C'mon, Jackie, or you're gonna be late." He reached down and grabbed her playfully, holding her in a headlock so she couldn't move. High school humor, boy-girl stuff for the Clearasil set.

"Hey," Jackie protested, trying to pull loose. "What are you doing?"

"Whatsa matter?" demanded Tony, laughing. "You don't like affection?"

A sister, thought Jackie. *He treats me like a little sister.* The thought hurt.

They walked down the stairway to the street and turned the corner toward Amsterdam Avenue, walking up Eighty-third Street.

"You know, today was definitely nowhere," said Tony. "And what's really bad is that it ain't even over yet." He shook his head sadly, and Jackie gave his arm a sympathetic little squeeze.

"Y'know that Paul somebody . . . I don't know his name . . . that choreographer who's got it in for me?"

"I know who you mean," Jackie nodded.

"No, you don't."

"Believe me, I know who you mean!" Jackie's voice rose in exasperation. Tony could be so stubborn! Sometimes she could just scream!

"C'mon, Jackie, don't get aggressive here. I don't want the public eavesdroppin' on my problems *here* . . ." Tony waved one hand at a small group of Puerto Rican kids who were paying them no attention at all. "So this guy's bad mouthin' me like I was a disease and should have my feet cut off or somethin'."

"What were you doing?" Jackie recognized that note in Tony's voice. It meant he'd been stubborn again at the audition. Doing things his own way.

Tony shrugged. "Nothin'. Dancin' the way I felt it, that's all." He turned to look Jackie earnestly in the face. Tony knew what her silence implied, that it was somehow his fault. If he'd toed the line and been a good little boy, he might have gotten the job. Well, who knows? Maybe so. But something always seemed to stand between him and the thing he wanted most. His shoulders sagged, and the corners of his expressive mouth turned down.

"Maybe it's an omen thing, that it's never gonna happen," he said gloomily.

"You don't believe that," Jackie said softly, her eyes on his.

"Why not? D'ya think makin' it is a sure thing? I mean, ya don't even know for sure if it's ever gonna pay off, do ya?" He left her side to take a few steps ahead of her, then turned to face her, talking as he walked. "Let me turn around. I talk better goin' backward. This way it hits ya straight in the face instead of havin' ta curve around."

"Oh, that's definitely better." Jackie smiled. "Now, what were you saying?" Inside, though, her heart was aching for him. Poor Tony! He could dance, no question about that. He could dance better than most of the men dancers in her show, better than *all* of them, in fact. Yet he was always his own worst enemy. That stubborn streak in him . . . and that *hunger*. Show business was full of sharks, circling the waters, sniffing for that hunger. Show them how much you wanted something, and they'd zero in and tear you to pieces.

"Just that I wouldn't mind if I could see that I was headin' somewhere."

". . . If you knew where you wanted to go," Jackie put in quickly.

Tony's mouth set in a stubborn line. "I know where I want to go."

"Sometimes you do," Jackie nodded agreement seriously, "but most of the time you lose sight of it."

Tony looked at her, a little startled. "And you're gonna tell me how I do that?"

But Jackie was shaking her head. "You don't want to hear it."

"Lose sight of what? C'mon!" Tony leaned forward, still walking backward, trying to peer into Jackie's eyes, but she evaded his glance.

He stopped and put a hand on her arm, urging her to look at him. At last she did, and her clear green eyes were shadowed, thoughtful and a little troubled.

"It's just . . ." she reached for the words. "It's just that you never go all the way when you dance. It's like you're holding back, afraid to let people see what you've really got."

This was an entirely new idea to Tony, and he drew back, astonished and a little angry.

"And why would I be afraid?" he asked Jackie stiffly.

"Because if you show them all you can do and they don't buy it, you'd probably think you never really had it and turn off dancing for good." Her little face was glowing with sincerity.

"Give me a break!" Tony backed off, his hands in the air in playful surrender. But Jackie was on a roll now and was not to be turned aside. She'd waited a long time to say this, and she wanted Tony to hear it.

"And by not doing what you can *really* do, you always have got an out. You can always say that you could have got the job if you really wanted it, if you made the commitment."

"Commitment?" Tony was stung by the word.

"Right," said Jackie forcefully. "Tony, you're good, you don't need any excuses. And if you don't get every job, so what? Just think that it's *their* loss, not yours. Because it *is!*" She gave him a dazzling smile, full of love mingled with sympathy.

But Tony was still hung up on a word. "You don't think I make commitments?" he asked, his mouth tight.

They had reached Jackie's apartment building now, a rundown five-story building, almost a tenement, yet the landlord still managed to charge outrageous rentals for minimal space.

"Not yet, I don't. I'm going to be late for the show. Do you have your key?"

Tony reached into his pocket for his key to Jackie's front door. "You haven't given anybody else a key, have you?" he asked, only half teasingly.

Putting her head to one side, Jackie smiled up at him.

"What kind of question is that?"

Tony grinned. "It's a key question all right," he cracked. "Have ya?" He unlocked the street door for her.

"What do you think?" Jackie parried the question with one of her own.

"I don't think so, but who knows?"

"*I* know," laughed the girl. Then almost hesitantly, not wanting to appear too eager, she asked as casually as she could, "Are you coming over tonight?"

Tony took a step backward, immediately on his guard. "I don't know, let me think about it." Then when he saw the expression on Jackie's face, disappointment mixed with a certain triumph as she'd proved her point, he broke into a lopsided grin. "Yeah, ya got a *commitment,*" and his voice underlined the word.

Then with a wave of his hand, he turned and walked away.

But for the rest of the day, his memory dragged him reluctantly back to what Jackie had thrown at him. Afraid to let himself go. Afraid to make a commitment. Afraid to show them what he had. Afraid. Afraid. Afraid. He, Tony Manero, had never been afraid of anything in his life!

So why did Jackie's words bother him so, as though a nerve had been struck?

Chapter Three

BY NIGHTFALL MOST OF TONY'S DEPRES-
sion had evaporated, thanks to his natural optimism
and good-humored ebullience. Also a nap and a
shower hadn't done him any harm either. He ran down
the three flights of stairs in the cheapo apartment hotel
he called home and came back ten minutes later with a
small pizza, steaming hot, and an iced Coke. These he
proceeded to demolish hungrily and thirstily, while he
dressed with care for the night's work ahead of him.

He shaved his face closely, checking out his jawline
and the corners of his eyes until he was satisfied that
he didn't look older than his twenty-four years. Then
he got into his working clothes—black tuxedo pants
that fitted him like lizard's skin fits a lizard. Around his
slim, tight waist he fastened a dark red cummerbund,
after tucking in the tails of a ruffled evening shirt. Over
this a waistcoat similar to a riverboat gambler's
hugged his chest snugly. Dressed, if not to kill, at least
to maim.

About a year after Tony had crossed that famous bridge, it dawned on him that a boy with his looks, charm and personality didn't have to scrub plates or push garment center hand trucks for a living. Most of the actors and dancers he met worked in restaurants and bars, where the tips were better than anything he could earn honestly elsewhere. The work was hard, but Tony was young and strong, and the hours were strange enough to allow him to attend classes and make it to auditions. He found work almost right away in one of those cutie-pie East Side singles bars—all hanging plants and imitation Tiffany lamps—that crowd elbow to elbow along Second Avenue. Three months later he lost the job, when it became obvious to his boss that the female patrons of Fuzzywuzzy were more interested in the handsome waiter than in the male paying customers. Tony's second job as a waiter vanished when the recession hit the New York restaurant scene, and tables were standing empty. But he had managed to hang on to his gig as one of the night bartenders at The Savage Instinct.

Opened in late '81 as competition for Xenon, just as Xenon had been competition for Studio 54, The Savage Instinct after a rather slow start had mushroomed into a big success, *the* hot place to dance. Instead of recorded music like other discos used, The Instinct boasted live rock bands, some of them actually not bad at all. The night that Mick Jagger had dropped in wearing Jerry Hall on his arm was the apogee of the club's popularity; after that it began to decline somewhat. But it still attracted a good-looking crowd of models, recording executives and a few of the Kennedy offspring.

The Instinct was big, no, biiiiiiiggggg. It had once

been a warehouse with a vast interior space. On the outside it still looked like a warehouse, squatting low and grim on a West Fifties side street, close to Eleventh Avenue. There wasn't even a neon sign outside announcing its presence; that was part of the mystique. If you weren't sure how to find it, it meant that you weren't in the know and therefore not welcome to dance there. But inside The Savage Instinct was state of the art, an explosion of sound and light that rocked the senses, deafened the ears, blinded the eyes and made the toes start tapping. The club's expenditure for Mylar alone would have fed a village in Bangladesh for a month. The lighting effects were computerized, and the permutations seemingly endless. The dance floor, ringed with lights, was vast enough not to seem overcrowded even when it was. Around the club were platforms of varying heights on which low benches padded in velvet and velvet floor cushions surrounded legless tables. On any night of the week all the tables were booked, and every bench and cushion filled by trim, expensively dressed behinds.

Tony was usually on the eleven–to–three shift, and he loved it. That's when the club was most alive, throbbing with hot music and the whirling forms of dancing bodies. There was an excitement, a feverish search for pleasure that excited Tony's senses and brought a sparkle to his blue eyes. He was happy to be a part of it, even though it meant standing on his feet without a break for four solid hours. He didn't mind the noise or the cigarette smoke or the constant demand for drinks. The tips were good, and there were fringe benefits.

A couple of the fringe benefits were perched on barstools even now, waiting for Tony to come back with the glasses. Although they were friends and not sisters, the two of them—Linda and Cathy With No Last Names—resembled each other so much they'd been taken for twins more than once. Both girls were twenty, with tight little bodies. Both wore their hair frizzed and streaked and were dressed in the fashion of the minute—fifties capri pants, tight in the butt, worn with oversize sweatshirts dotted with rhinestones, three-inch heels on their ankle-strap shoes. They were sipping Campari and Perrier-with-a-twist slowly, making their drinks last for economy's sake and eyeing the men around them, checking out the possibilities. But it was Tony Manero they were really waiting for.

Expertly balancing a heavy tray filled with dirty glasses, Tony walked briskly up to the bar and set the tray down. Fred Harris was behind the bar; he and Tony worked the same shift on the same nights. A medium-height burly man, Fred was a likable guy, but mean when crossed.

"Hey, Fred, you got that next order ready?" asked Tony, moving the glasses off the tray and into the sink.

"Right here," said Fred. There was a tight, slightly sour set to his mouth as he added, "Looks like some of your groupie friends are here."

"What?" Tony looked puzzled.

Jerking his chin toward the No-Last-Name Twins, Fred sneered, "Those things. They friends of yours?"

Tony swiveled his head for a look, then nodded. "Passin' acquaintances. So what?"

"So how about sharing the wealth?"

Tony grinned. "What am I, your booking agent?" It always amused him how jealous other guys got. There were so many women in the world, more than enough to go around, or so it seemed to him. Why get greedy?

"You don't wanna share?" Fred grinned back, but his eyes were shadowed. "Who cares? I don't need your hand-me-downs."

Tony raised one eyebrow. "Whaddya got, emotional problems tonight or what?"

But Fred turned his back on him, angry with himself for letting Tony see that he was jealous. It was just that every woman in the place with any claims to a halfway decent face and body turned on to Manero; anybody would be tired of it by now, but Manero seemed to eat it up and ask for more. It made him, Fred, sick to his stomach.

Shrugging, Tony went to wash the glasses. No skin off him if Fred wanted to get mad.

"Hi ya, Tony." Cathy and Linda had slid over a couple of stools and were perched directly in front of him.

"How ya doin'?" Tony greeted them. It embarrassed him a little to be seen with his hands in the dishwater. Not so hot for his macho image.

"How late you working tonight?" Cathy asked him directly.

"Till three."

"Wanna come over?" No "How are you, how's things?" Straight to business. What happened to old-fashioned courtesy?

Tony's brows contracted in a frown. "I don't know," he muttered into the dishwater, shaking his head slightly.

"What's wrong?" demanded Cathy.

Tony looked at her frankly. "Nothin', except the last time I came over, I almost left with brain damage," he told the girl bluntly. "You guys party too hard. You oughtta be a tag team."

Linda giggled lasciviously. "Good guys are hard to find."

"Even if they got dishpan hands," Cathy threw in sarcastically.

Stung, Tony pulled his hands out of the water. "Hey," he countered defensively, "the fact is I really like doin' this 'cause it keeps my nails real clean." Reaching over the bar, he grabbed Cathy's wrist and dragged her hand down into the water. "Here, you try it!"

Cathy let out a little yip of mingled fear and delight as her hand plunged into the soapy water. Tony's grip held her wrist in a cuff of iron, and his blue eyes were blazing, star sapphires. It really turned her on, and she smiled deeply into Tony's eyes.

At once he let her go. It gave him a creepy feeling, the way girls came on with him sometimes. Like they were using him for their pleasure, like he was a . . . a . . . thing, instead of a person. It wasn't natural. It never occurred to Tony that what he believed was natural was that men could behave that way with women, not women with men. His Bay Ridge boyhood had not allowed for any sensitivity, so sensitivity had never been Tony Manero's strong point. What also had never occurred to him was that there might be something *between* being a star and an assistant bartender, something worth having. For Tony Manero there was no middle ground; go for broke, take it all.

What he was now, a kid scrambling to make it, working his tail off at any kind of job he could scrounge, getting cut at auditions, all that was due to change. Meanwhile Tony got his kicks when and where he could.

He liked simple things. Good food, sexy women, a chance to dance. That redheaded model sitting there with the old dude with the gray hair. He'd seen her in commercials and on magazine covers. She was a ten, a definite ten, maybe even an eleven. The old guy with her looked like he had bucks. Big bucks. He was wearing a gold watch as thin as a razor blade with a long French name. Six thousand smackers. Tony had seen it in Cartier's window on Fifth Avenue. Someday he'd have a watch like that. Meanwhile the model was looking at Tony as if she were starving and he were roast beef. He could feel those long gray eyes like laser beams piercing his body at various strategic points.

It made him feel good, it boosted his confidence, but it made him feel bad too. It reminded him that instead of sitting across from a woman as desirable and foxy as this, wearing a six-thousand dollar watch, he was serving her drinks and taking away the dirty glasses. Maybe he could get to borrow a girl like that, but he was still in no position to keep her.

The music was building, and the dancing was getting wilder. Tony took a minute to watch the floor. He longed to be out on it, wearing a new shirt, new shoes, showing off his moves. Rock and roll pounded in his ears and poured down his body to his feet. Lotta good dancers out there shakin' it, but Tony knew there was nobody on the floor who came near him.

Unless . . . who was that guy? Tall, dark, well dressed, he reminded Tony of himself. He moved with confidence, as though he owned the floor. He was dancing with a long-legged beauty whose hair whipped around like rainfall in the wind, but the girl's slim beauty was only an ornament to show the young man off even more strongly. Arrogant, graceful, he was worth looking at and he knew it. Tony was unaware that his hands had knotted into fists of frustration and envy. Here he was, stuck, making with the ice cubes and the lemon peel and the Ivory Liquid, and that stud was gliding across the floor like it belonged to him, fancy dancing right under Tony's nose. When would it be *his* turn?

Tony turned at a tap on his shoulder, a question mark on his face. Cathy was standing there, one hand on her hip in a presumably provocative pose, smiling at him. In the background Linda, who had never had much to say, stood watching and waiting.

"We on later?" challenged Cathy.

Tony shook his head, his gaze wandering back to the dance floor.

"I can't make it."

"Why not?" Cathy's gaze followed his, puzzled. Who was he looking at?

" 'Cause lately I'm career oriented," Tony told her impatiently.

"And what's that supposed to mean?" The girl was getting angry; nothing she counted on seemed to be happening for her.

"It means I don't have time for meaningful relationships right now," Tony said, half-sarcastically, half-humorously. He didn't want to hurt anybody's feelings, but he wanted both of them to go away.

"That right?" Cathy's eyes narrowed, and the corners of her mouth turned down. "Let me tell you something," she continued through gritted teeth, "guys like you aren't relationships. You're exercise!"

And with this parting shot, a good one, she turned and marched off, her little butt twitching, and Linda trailing behind her.

Tony stood rubbing his neck, more wounded than

he'd admit to himself. That was twice today he'd been zinged but good. An embarrassed grin spread over his features, and he hoped that nobody had overheard Cathy's crack. Unlikely in this noise, but you never knew. The grin faded quickly as Barry Kerstein, the owner of The Savage Instinct, came up fast, anger making his gold chains bounce on his neck. Sweat was standing out on his forehead and making little wet beads under his toupee.

"What are you doing?" he demanded. "No mixing with the customers. You know the policy, so what the hell areya doing? That's five minutes you owe me."

Tony gave Barry his blankest expression. "I owe everybody else, so why not you, right?" Turning on his heel, he walked off without another word, hearing Barry yelling at him behind his back, "Don't be wise!"

Tony stalked back to the bar and grabbed up another tray of drinks. On the floor Cathy was dancing now. That tall cat was still boogying, music in his soul and pouring out of his feet. Everybody had come here to dance, and everybody was dancing. Everybody but Tony Manero. Depression, black and enveloping, began to seep through his body, making him tired. Suddenly the music was too loud, the lights too blinding, the gaiety was forced, and the hour was late. Tony felt a headache coming on; he wished it were closing time.

It came eventually, closing time, and Tony cleaned up quickly, wanting to be out of there. He hit the streets at about three-twenty; the December night was cold but sparkling clear and there was a high frigid moon. He had intended to walk home and go directly to bed, but his fingers closed around a key in his pocket, and he changed his mind. This was no time to be alone; what he needed was somebody warm lying next to him, somebody who thought of him as something more than just a piece of meat or a pair of working hands.

Summoning a cab with a loud whistle, he gave the driver Jackie Call's address.

Her apartment was a large Upper West Side studio room, and one where a young woman definitely lived. Jackie's taste was reflected in the plants and in the simple, comfortable furniture. On the big, floppy comfortable chair was a buttercup yellow pillow that Jackie had made herself. On it was needlepointed To Dance Is to Live; To Live Is to Dance. Above the head of the sofa hung a large poster stating Dance Is the Only Art Wherein We Ourselves Are the Stuff of Which It Is Made. Above and below that quotation ran a series of smaller quotes: Dancing Is Silent Poetry. The Material for the Dance Is Air, the Movement Is Breath and the Source Is Love. A Dancer Ought to Be Light as a Flame. Dance Is Life at Its Most Glorious Moment. He Who Cannot Dance Puts the Blame on the Floor, and so on. Tony had read that poster a hundred times or more, and he was sick of it. Fortune cookie stuff.

Dance Is a Pain in the Legs and an Ache in the Gut, that's what Jackie should embroider on a pillow, thought Tony. *Dance Makes Your Thighs Thick and Your Wallet Thin*. That was a good one; he'd have to remember that. He was no less depressed than when he came, only now he was itchy at the amount of time he seemed to be losing. Time, somebody told him once, was invented to keep bad things from happening to you all at once, but Tony didn't believe it. Time was the enemy.

Life was dancing by him double-time, and he was still fooling around in a dance studio and a bar. When would it be his turn? When he was eighty? Hell with that!

Gotta stop wasting time. Gotta make a positive move. His restlessness woke Jackie up.

She sat yawning, leaning on one elbow. Her short yellow hair was all tousled, and Tony resisted putting his hand on her shaggy little head.

"When did you get here? Why do you have to go now?"

"It's five o'clock," countered Tony.

"Stay for breakfast." It was almost a plea, but it stopped just short of one, as though Jackie understood that a plea would do her no good at all.

"I'm not hungry."

"What's wrong, Tony?" asked Jackie quietly.

Frustration twisted Tony's face into a mask of anguish.

"I gotta get somethin' goin'. I'm wastin' everything, ya know?"

"No, you're not," Jackie told him quietly but firmly.

But Tony still kept shaking his head. "I gotta get goin'," he said gruffly and headed for the apartment door.

"I'll miss you," Jackie called softly after him.

Tony turned, still scowling. "Don't have to say that," he told her in an embarrassed mutter.

Wrapping her arms around her uptucked knees, Jackie lowered her head so that Tony couldn't see tears beginning to form in her eyes. "It's . . . it's just the way I feel," she said quietly, biting her lip. "You don't have to say anything."

For a long moment in time, Tony stood frozen. Part of him wanted her to cry so that he could cry with her and their tears would be the glue that would bond them together. But the rest of him, and by far the larger part, stood there puzzled and slightly angry; what the hell did she want from him?

He was acutely uncomfortable—part embarrassment, part guilt—and all he really knew was that he wanted out of there, and fast.

"I'll see ya later," he told her briskly and pulled the door shut behind him. Immediately he felt better, as though he could breathe more easily. He was never comfortable in the presence of emotion; why did things always have to get heavy? Hey, he liked Jackie, right? Didn't she understand that? Why did she think he was with her at all if he didn't have some kind of feeling for her?

As to what kind of feeling or how much . . . why did chicks always wanna talk about it? Why couldn't they stay cool like guys? Even so a faint twinge of guilt did gnaw at him. It was good to see her face over the morning cup of coffee. So why had he bugged out? There was an impatience eating at him, not letting him be still. The whole damn day had been one long downer. First the audition with its humiliating rejections, then the hassles at The Savage Instinct and the phony faces who were always there, always on the make. So he had gone to Jackie for a little peace, a little quiet, and she'd given it to him freely and without stint. Even so he'd cut out as soon as he could. His private demons were pursuing him again, the ones who kept whispering in his ear that it was getting late, he was getting old, he was gonna be left out, passed over, ignored. Whenever he heard their evil little voices hissing in whispers, he had to get up and move.

The streets were icy cold; dawn was still a good half hour away, and he was maybe a good half mile from his hotel, but he wanted to walk, *needed* to walk. He needed the fresh cold air to clear his head a little; he needed the activity of fast, strenuous walking to empty his brain of all the doubts that were plaguing it.

He turned up the collar of his jacket against the wind, plunged his hands in his pockets and headed down Broadway, going downtown.

Behind him he left the complications of loving and a thin blond girl crying into her pillow.

Chapter Four

By THE TIME TONY HAD WALKED THE TEN blocks downtown and was turning west on Seventy-third Street, the morning light had broken, and the sun was struggling to come out. The air was chilly, and as the light grew stronger, the sound of birds twittering and chirping filled the almost empty streets. Something about their cheerful morning greetings made Tony almost smile, but he suppressed it.

Even if he had been smiling, the sight of Tony's hotel would have chased away the last trace of merriment. Outside near the entrance a handful of wobbly winos, their faces gray with stubble and ill health, crouched huddled against the wintry cold of morning. These bums were not even together enough to make it over to any of the rundown men's shelters, which would supply them with a flop for a night complete with bedbugs and fleas. The furthest distance this lot traveled was to drag themselves over to Grand Central Station, where the Salvation Army had set up a mobile soup kitchen. So at least once a day, they ate a hot meal. The rest of the time they panhandled passersby until they'd gotten together the price of a cheap pint of sweet fortified wine, which they shared among themselves like a band of brothers. Scraps of food, cigarette butts, yesterday's newspapers to keep their shriveled bodies warm—all these were available free, one needed only to bend down into the gutter and pick it up. The sight of these pieces of human wreckage trembling in the biting cold of a city morning in late winter gave Tony the shivers himself. He felt a mingled revulsion and pity for the wasted lives of these men, although he would have denied to himself and the rest of the world that pity was what he felt.

Giving them a wide berth, he came into his hotel lobby. The Forsythe had never been grand, not even when it was new. Built in 1911, it had been intended to be a moderately priced family hotel, conveniently located, if not in the heart of Manhattan, then surely in its kidney. Not luxurious, it had been nonetheless clean, comfortable and relatively modern. But that was 1911, and this was seventy-two years later. The Forsythe had fallen on evil times and even now was waiting fearfully for the coming of the wrecker's ball, since everyone knew that the seedy old neighborhoods of the Upper West Side were undergoing what the newspapers called a "renaissance by gentrification."

Now The Forsythe rented rooms by the week and even a few by the hour to the local hookers. All you got was a place to flop, a nonworking sink in your room, a creaky iron bedstead, a window shade with holes in it and a rickety chair that held a pile of laundry. What passed for a bureau was an ancient cardboard relic with warped drawers. And that was it. No private bath, no shower, no toilet; a single bulb on a ratty string hung down from the ceiling, giving out very dim light. Which was probably just as well, because you wouldn't want to look closely at the mattress or the sheets. Home sweet home, eighty-five bucks a week.

The lobby was a mass of peeling wallpaper and scuffed linoleum floors. The shabby floor ashtrays, filled with dirty sand, old cigar butts and cigarette ends, hadn't been emptied within living memory. Off to the side against the far wall was the desk clerk's cubicle, where in 1911 husbands and wives and drummers from out of state used to sign their names with a flourish in the registry book. But the book had long ago bitten the dust; nobody had signed in or out of The Forsythe since World War II.

Behind the desk an old man sat snoring, his head thrown back to expose his toothless gums. Hair sprouted from his ears and nostrils, and his Adam's apple bobbled with every snore.

"Any messages?" asked Tony, then he grinned. There were never any messages, not for him, not for anybody else. He passed the old man on tiptoe, unwilling to disturb him.

Tony stood in the doorway, surveying his twelve-foot by seven-foot domain. The room was noisy with the sound of hissing steam; the radiator had a faulty valve. Not only couldn't you shut the thing off, but boiling hot water streamed out of it and had turned the forty-year-old mud-colored carpet into a mildewed and smelly mess.

Tony shook his head, marveling. He never ceased to wonder how a place could get to look this bad, or what he was doing here. He'd tried to get his room together more than once, but it was a hopeless task that defied all his efforts. Because there was no closet in the room, Tony had driven a straight line of nails into the walls over the management's protests to provide pegs for the hangers on which his clean clothing hung neatly. Clothing was very important to Tony; he took enormous pride in his personal appearance, and no matter how difficult the circumstances, he showered twice a day every day.

Now he scooped up the laundry on the chair, grabbed his soap and his dop kit with his toothpaste and razor, and made his way down the hall to the hotel bathroom, which served eight tenants. Because of the earliness of the hour, the place was blessedly empty, and Tony had the chance to take a long shower while washing his socks and underwear, his dance clothes and a couple of shirts in the shower with him. Like everything else at The Forsythe, the shower had seen better days. The nozzle dripped and drizzled rather than ran, and the color of the water was on occasion indescribable, yet Tony managed to emerge from the bathroom forty-five minutes later clean, shaved and carrying his wet laundry. Now he felt better.

By the time he'd strung his wash up on the make-shift clotheslines he had strung around his miniscule room, he was bushed. It had been a long day and a longer night, and he needed a few hours' sleep. Stretching himself out on his narrow bed, he closed his eyes.

When he opened them again, it was full morning. About eight-thirty. He swung his legs to the floor and sat up. The depression had passed. Today was a working day, just like any other. Time to take care of business. Tony dressed with care, singing along to the top song played by the Top Forty station on his little transistor. When he was looking sharp enough for his liking, Tony took a step backward and did a little dance turn. Then he picked up an envelope filled with his head shots and headed out into the world.

The old buzzard was still at the desk in the lobby, minimally awake.

"Any messages?" Tony asked automatically, and just as automatically, the ancient geezer shook his head no.

The subway was bopping, teeming with life. He got off at Times Square. The reason Tony spent so much time in the shadow of Times Square rather than up-town closer to Jackie was that he wanted to be near show biz. This was the theater district, the side streets crowded with the Broadway theaters of legend—the

Morosco, the Royale, the Shubert, the Winter Garden, the Majestic. On these streets had sung and danced the greatest in the history of the musical theater—Ethel Merman, Gertrude Lawrence, Ray Bolger, Bob Fosse, Carol Haney, Fred Astaire, Gwen Verdon, Lauren Bacall, Ben Vereen, Angela Lansbury, Ann Reinking, Carol Channing, Barbra Streisand—the list is endless, inspiring and endless. Someday Tony Manero's name would be added to that list, alongside Gower Champion's and Gregory Hines's. Meanwhile just to walk down these streets gave him a thrill.

Tony shouldered his way past the nickel-and-dime drug dealers and the twenty-dollars-a-pop three-card monte sharpsters; Times Square was as full of these entrepreneurs as it was of hookers, porno shops, video arcades and greasy fried chicken stands. They were part of the color. They made New York what it was, hustling, brawling, smelly, dangerous, exciting and strangely phosphorescent, especially in daylight. You had to be made of strong stuff to survive here, let alone to thrive.

Tony's destination was one of the oldest skyscrapers on Broadway. It was a building that long ago had housed song writers and music publishers. Now it was almost entirely given over to agents. Not the slick, expensively tailored and carefully barbered talent agents whose offices are on the thirty-third floor and who have access to WATS lines, a telex number, mail rooms, Xerox machines and all the status and convenience of the new technology. No, *those* agents handled only the top attractions and made the biggest deals. *These* were agents who operated on the fringes, who sent unknowns over to off-Broadway auditions or came up with a drummer and a piano man for an engagement in a Teaneck, New Jersey lounge. It wasn't Tony's intention to stay with this class of agent for long. But to get with this class of agent, or *any* class of agent, was a necessity. Up to now he'd struck out. But with this new determination he was feeling and his new head shot and résumé, which had taken a two hundred and fifty dollar bite out of his meager resources, he was almost confident enough to try again.

Quickly running down the names on the folded list he took from his jacket pocket, Tony entered the building lobby and consulted the directory board. The names were there. He decided to start with the upper floors and work his way down through the building. Always start at the top, he told himself bravely, although he was actually feeling far from brave.

Wolfe & Wolfe was on the seventeenth floor, a venerable agency that went back to vaudeville. Photographs of the great and the near-great lined the walls of the reception room. Presumably these were clients of Wolfe & Wolfe, although no actual claims were made.

Tony asked for Wolfe and was denied. He was denied the second Wolfe too, or in fact an audience with anybody in the firm. Well, what the hell. He took his photograph carefully out of the manila envelope he was carrying—these pictures were called "head shots"—and laid it gently on the receptionist's desk.

"I'm, y'know, a dancer by nature," he told her hopefully. "Been studying for four years and now I teach. But I want you to know I'm very available for TV work."

The receptionist, bored, nodded without looking at Tony's photo or résumé. Tony left with the knowledge that his precious, costly picture was destined for the old circular file, the wastebasket.

From Wolfe & Wolfe he worked his way down through Abrams & Jennings, Kaminsky & Light, Snyder Associates, The Busch Group. Not once did he get past the front desk; not once did he penetrate the outer office with its Styrofoam paper cups and greasy donut wrappers, its hopefuls sitting on the outer benches, endlessly waiting for an appointment.

Having worked his way from the top to the bottom of the Agmore Building, a discouraged Tony turned his steps westward to the haunts of the even-lesser agents, the guys with only a handful of clients, with plastic plants in the outer offices, ugly secretaries and low overhead. Here too he delivered his spiel in vain: "Available for any kind of modeling jobs, acting parts, dramatic parts, comedy parts, repertory, melodramas, and I believe I'm certainly available for musicals, soap operas, road shows, print ads." His smile was getting feebler, and the sparkle in his blue eyes was definitely fading, but still he'd haul out his photograph and add, "Voice-overs, any radio work. Are ya looking for the healthy outdoor type? I'm okay at some sports like pushups and stickball, running. And if it's absolutely necessary, I don't mind doing any kind of extra work. Anything, but no nudity. I promised my mother no nudity. Guess she's afraid I'll get a cold, but the fact is I'm a dancer by nature."

And in the face of all of this charm, enthusiasm, hope and eagerness, the only response Tony received was indifference, boredom, irritation.

Grudgingly the head shot and résumé were accepted in office after office, but it was apparent that no attention was going to be paid to either, and that no interest was available at all for Tony Manero, whoever he was.

It was enough to discourage Mother Teresa. It was enough to make any mortal give up. It was in short the hardest part of show business. The rejection—cold, impersonal, yet bitter with an undercurrent of gloating. You dragged yourself from one office to another on a smile and a shoeshine, looking your best, grinning your widest, offering your face and your body and your charm and what talent you might or might not possess, and somebody's secretary with a rat's eyes and a potato nose seemed to enjoy turning you down and showing you the door. Meanwhile every day you saw faces on TV and in the movies not equal to yours, lousy acting making big bucks, dancers in successful parts whom you could dance rings around. Only *they* had agents with clout, while *you* couldn't even get an agent without any. It wasn't fair, but it was show business.

Tony's feet were beginning to hurt from all the walking. He'd covered block after block from Forty-fifth Street up to Fifty-seventh, and now he turned into a small building west of Eighth Avenue on Fifty-eighth Street, a building so ratty and rundown that you couldn't imagine what kind of business would rent space here.

But the Milton Swartz Agency was last on Tony's list and the Milton Swartz Agency was on the third floor of this building. There was of course no elevator, and Tony half ran, half dragged himself to the third floor.

The glass on the office door hadn't been washed in decades, and it was difficult even to make out the firm's name, but it was there. Tony knocked.

After a second, a gruff voice came through the door. "Yeah? Whaddya want?"

"Tony Manero. Can I get an interview?" called Tony.

Behind the door he could hear scuffling and what sounded like muffled laughter, a woman's giggles. Then nothing. He waited a few seconds.

"Listen, I walked crosstown to see ya. Can ya look at my picture or something?"

Again a silence broken by muffled giggles, and the gruff voice answered. "Slide it under the door."

"What?" Tony couldn't believe his ears.

"Slide it under the door." The voice was impatient now, wanting to go back to whatever it was doing with or to the giggling lady.

Tony shrugged at nobody in particular and slid the precious photograph carefully under the door. For a minute or two there was complete silence, then Tony said hopefully, "Whaddya think? Am I right for anything?"

More suppressed giggling answered him, then the photograph was slid back out to him. But now it was badly crumpled—as though by a huge meaty hand— and totally worthless.

"Not interested," said the gruff voice on a note of finality.

Tony bent to pick up the crumpled picture and stood there in the badly lit shabby hallway, making automatic and futile smoothing motions with his hands. His brain was churning, his heart racing, his gut twisted with anger. Anger. Some yutz was in there putting the moves on Little Miss Nobody and didn't want to be disturbed. During business hours Mr. Hotshot Agent didn't want to be disturbed. Instead he had ruined a valuable piece of property that didn't belong to him.

Tony's hands balled into fists, crushing the photograph beyond recognition. His eyes glittered with rage. What he wanted to do was smash that office door open, catch the grunter and the giggler in the act and throw them down the stairs in their underwear. He could just see the looks of terror on their pudgy faces, hear the giggles rise into shrieks. It would serve them both right if the story hit the papers.

Drawing in a long deep breath, Tony fought to master himself and finally succeeded. What the hell good would it do him to smash open that door? Would it get him a job or send his career on its way? Maybe not, but it would hand him a yuk, and he needed a laugh right now. He turned to go, feeling lower than a snail's foot, lower than a catfish's gills, lower than anything you could name that was low-down. Lower than an agent.

When he came out onto the street again, he was locked tight in the grip of despondency. It seemed like nothing could break it. Not two slices of pizza at Ray's washed down by a Dr. Brown's Celery Tonic. Not even watching a Double Dutch tournament on the street near Lincoln Center made him smile, although the quickness and agility of the black teenagers who danced nimbly between the ropes was something he always got a kick out of. He thought briefly of Jackie, and he wanted her. Not to sleep with, but to talk to.

Stepping into a telephone booth, he dialed her number and prayed to Saint Jude that she was at home. She was and agreed to meet him "just for a walk." By the time he reached her front steps, she was waiting for him, dressed neatly in a cotton shirt, faded jeans and an old shetland sweater under a down jacket and looking like a morning in June. The sight of her brought a thin smile to Tony's face, even though it faded immediately.

Jackie could see that something was wrong, and it didn't need a crystal ball to figure out what that something was. The envelope in Tony's fingers dangling listlessly was a good clue. Tony had been out looking for show work, for an agent, and had come up empty.

It didn't take Jackie long to get Tony talking about it.

They walked slowly together side by side, and Tony's words came slowly, listlessly. It pained Jackie to hear him. Tony was usually electric with energy.

"Y'know, it's like you're invisible. They don't even see you. I don't know, they make you feel like you're just wasting their time. They all sound like my old man used to. 'Give it up and get yourself a regular job.' "

Jackie put one small hand on Tony's arm. "Tony," she began softly, "do you know what it gets down to?"

Tony flashed her a bitter smile. "Feelin' sorry for myself, right?"

But Jackie was shaking her head emphatically. "No, it gets down to only what *you* think. Do *you* think you're good?"

A slight shrug lifted Tony's shoulders an inch. "I

don't know . . . good enough, I guess . . ." he mumbled.

"More than enough," said Jackie firmly, tightening her grip on his arm. "So if you know that and believe it, how can you keep getting so down on yourself? You know what you can do!"

Tony whirled on her suddenly. "What about you?" he demanded.

"What about me?" Jackie looked bewildered.

"Yeah. You've been in and outta chorus lines for six years, doin' the same as everybody else. Don't you want to do something that's all *you?*"

The way that Tony had changed the subject when it got too uncomfortable for him to handle made Jackie smile, but she let him get away with it.

"If it happens, good," she said mildly. "If it doesn't, it won't bother me."

Tony's bright blue eyes widened. "How can you think like that?" he demanded.

Now it was Jackie's turn to shrug lightly. "You don't have to; I do." she smiled.

"What's that supposed to mean?"

Jackie didn't allow herself to get ruffled. "You know a woman's career as dancer is half as long as a man's," she reminded him. "So the chances of making it are half as many, right? I've got to be real with myself, right? Anyway, will you come to see the show tonight? Tonight's supposed to be the last performance."

Tony hesitated. This had been an unspoken bone of contention between them for the six months that Jackie had been dancing in *Perdita,* a Broadway hit that had run for several years and won Tonys. For some reason he had never gone to see her dance; you'd think a friend would turn out to see a friend on stage, but Tony couldn't seem to bring himself to do it. Jackie had never nagged him about it, but it was plain to see that she was hurt and felt let down.

"I don't think I can make it," he said, a little lamely.

"Why do you keep making excuses?" asked Jackie calmly.

Tony had no answer for this, so he turned to split, his customary way of avoiding unpleasant confrontations. He just walked away from them.

But Jackie wasn't about to let that happen.

"C'mon, Tony," she said, stopping him with a hand on his arm. "Don't. Don't have this competition thing with me," she pleaded.

That hit a nerve. "What competition?" Tony demanded hotly, his cheeks burning. "Why? Because you're in the show and I'm not? That's not competition!"

"What is it then?" asked Jackie with a soft smile.

Tony paused a minute. Then, "Envy!" he blurted out honestly, and they both laughed, friends again.

"Will you be there?" urged Jackie gently.

Tony waved a deprecating hand. "I got all these commitments. You know, business meetings." It was the poorest excuse for a lie, and both of them knew it.

Jackie shook her head at him as she would have at a small naughty boy. "Anyway, if you can get out of all those business meetings, I'll leave a ticket at the box office."

Tony turned to leave her, but a scowl spread over his handsome features and he turned back. "I can pay for my own ticket," he told her stiffly.

Recognizing that she had hurt him unintentionally, Jackie only nodded. As she watched him walk off, a tall, well-made figure with none of the usual bounce in his step, Jackie felt a pang of sympathy for him. Poor Tony! He tried so hard and got so nowhere! Was there really a future for Tony? Would he ever make it? If only he didn't take everything so *personally!* What Tony Manero needed was a large portion of objectivity; maybe that would dull the pain of his daily grind a little. She sighed. All that energy, and too much of it wasted on anger and self-pity.

Chapter Five

He'd intended to get to the theater in time to see the entire show, but so much for good intentions. Sleep had overcome him, the heavy sleep of mental exhaustion, of bitterness, hopes unfulfilled, and he had slept until a quarter hour past the time the curtain went up. With barely enough time to grab a quick shower under the rusty nozzle and throw on some clothes, Tony arrived at the Royale in time to see the audience thronging the lobby for intermission. Well, at least he'd get to watch the second half.

Perdita had been a monster hit and had been running for over two years. Jackie had been dancing with the show for about six months and was still filled with enthusiasm and delight. She had been hurt, really hurt, when Tony hadn't shown up to catch her on stage, but after six months the hurt had softened to a kind of wry understanding. It was painful for Tony to accept the success of anybody he knew—especially Jackie—when he was having none of his own. Still, closing night was special, and she did want him to be there.

Instead of taking his seat after intermission, Tony

wandered backstage, greeting a handful of younger people he knew casually, and took up a station in the wings, where he could watch the action and still feel at home. Being backstage meant you were in show business; it was different from sitting in a paid-for seat, even a privileged house seat.

The curtain was up again, and the orchestra was playing the show's big hit as overture to the second half. The ballad had already been reprised three times, but the audience could not get enough of the song; Streisand, Neil Diamond, Frank Sinatra had all recorded it. And now the music was turning from romantic to funky, and the chorus darted onto the stage costumed as foxes, complete with pointed ears and long brushes for tails.

Tony spotted Jackie immediately. She was good, damn good. She ought to be dancing leads, not chorus parts. The dance itself was clever and tricky, requiring the dancers to run, leap and hide, all from invisible dogs who never did show up on stage. Still it was evident that the audience was entirely with the foxes, gasping at the most daring of the leaps. The dance had energy and originality; Tony was beginning to be sorry that he'd missed the first act.

He took a surreptitious look at his program. It was time for the big production number. The curtain had fallen on the foxes, who had scampered off into the opposite wings, so that Tony hadn't had a chance to congratulate Jackie. Now a simple pas de deux was being danced "in one," which meant in front of the fallen curtain, giving the cast a chance to change into the next costume and the stagehands a chance to get the production number set ready. Whenever you see an act "in one," you can hear the rumbling of the stage machinery and the footsteps of the technical crew going on behind it.

At last the two dancers made their exit to scattered applause, and the curtain rose on a totally dark stage. The music was low and sensual, mostly woodwinds, with a dark-voiced oboe carrying the melody and soft clarinets wailing sadly behind it.

One spotlight, one, and a gasp from the audience as a face of extraordinary beauty rose from the darkness. Tony was unaware that he too had let out his breath, astonished by the girl's loveliness. Huge eyes—he couldn't see the color of them—delineated by arched slender brows, a pouting mouth with slightly raised upper lip. Her hair, a cloud of tangled silk, and an expression on her face sultry enough to burn paper. The spotlight widened, revealing the dancer's body, and the clarinets' voices rose in a passionate lament. High breasts, narrow waist and incredibly long legs, slim, yet with powerful muscles in the thighs. A devilish body, a disciplined body, a dancer's body.

Tony stood awestruck; the intensity of the girl's beauty moved him beyond words. He was unaware of anything else. When she began to dance with her partner, a sexual duet, Tony could only envision himself in the male dancer's place. It was *he* dancing with her, bending her low so that the tangled mass of her incredible hair touched the stage floor. It was he turning her body around to meet his, holding her waist in his eager hands. He barely saw the rest of the dancers take the stage, was barely aware that the dance was building into the production number climax of the show. He didn't even see Jackie. All he saw was this tawny young woman center stage, and he felt in the marrow of his bones that he was destined to know her, to love her, and that they would change each other's lives. He tore his eyes away from her only long enough to consult his program. Laura Ravell, it said, "featured dancer Laura Ravell."

Laura. Laura Ravell. It suited her, it was right for her. Those *L*s and *R*s, soft sounds. He couldn't take his eyes off her. She was devastating. The dance was incredibly erotic, and the dancer was by turns alluring, defiant, subtly sensual and openly sexual. There wasn't anything she couldn't handle. She moved on the stage as though it belonged to her and only to her. And it did. Nobody up there was fit to share it with her. Only he, Tony. He felt as though they had been created to dance together. His body would be attuned to hers, in perfect rhythm with hers.

It was over. The show was over, the curtain coming down to thunderous applause. The dancers were rushing into the wings, breathless and sweating. They ran past Tony, and Laura was with them, but he didn't notice the gleam of her sweat or hear the panting of her breath. All he could see was her beauty, as overpowering up close as it was on stage. She moved past him without a glance, but his head turned as she went by, and his eyes remained glued to her until she disappeared into her dressing room.

"Tony! Tony!"

He dragged his head around slowly. It was Jackie, a radiant, exhilarated, exhausted and dripping Jackie.

"Do you hear that!? Listen to that sound!" she gasped, totally out of breath.

Tony grinned at her. "Yeah, it's definitely a lotta hands bangin' together," he acknowledged.

Jackie laughed, glowing with happiness and pride and the joy of seeing Tony standing there.

"Did you like it?"

"You looked great, Jackie."

Her bright little face lit up even more as she looked happily up at Tony. "Really?"

"Excellent," replied Tony, feeling like six kinds of heel. He'd barely noticed her on stage; his entire attention had been riveted on Laura Ravell.

"Thanks," she gasped. "I gotta change. Are you gonna stay around?" It was impossible for Jackie to keep the hoping out of her voice.

"Sure, why not," said Tony lightly, feeling even more of a rat than ever. It wasn't Jackie he wanted to stick around for. He had to lay eyes on Laura again.

"I thought you had all these *commitments*," teased Jackie.

Tony grinned down at her and spread his palms apart. "Gimme a break," he pleaded.

Jackie stood on tiptoe to kiss Tony on the cheek, then she ran off to the chorus dressing rooms. Tony turned around to look for Laura.

There she was, talking to a couple of guys in suits under the stairs near the dressing rooms. They had the unmistakable look of successful agents—polished and sleek and very well fed. The kind of men who feasted on money-talk, rolling every rich syllable around in their mouths like beads of caviar. To them Laura was not a woman, but a walking contract.

Tony stood looking at her, at the poised and confident way she was standing there, at the casual gesture with which she scooped her long hair up from the nape of her neck to cool it after her exertions. Her body was a sinuous length of female beauty; her long legs in their dancers' mesh stockings were the most shapely he'd ever seen. The woman was a total turn-on, and Tony stood fascinated, rooted to the spot.

At last the business discussion was over, and Laura broke away from the agents. Instantly Tony dashed forward in her direction. It was an instinctual action, but he had no idea of what he was going to say to her.

"Uh . . . excuse me," he began, almost bumping into her.

Her lustrous eyes widened. The color of them was honey to match the color of her hair. Her eyes were actually reddish gold, the color of old amber, and Tony had never seen anything like them before. She was looking expectantly at him now; there was no annoyance on her face. She was simply waiting to hear what he had to say.

"I . . . uh . . . I wanna say that you're an incredible dancer," said Tony in a rush.

A tiny smile threatened the corners of Laura's mouth.

"Thank you very much," she drawled in an accent

that Tony couldn't identify, but which entranced him instantly.

She looked up at him, seeing a tall, handsome boy in his midtwenties with an incredible body and two of the bluest eyes she'd ever encountered. There was a deep cleft in the boy's strong chin, a punctuation mark to his good looks. Thick dark hair tumbled over his brow; he was well worth looking at.

But she saw, too, a naiveté, an unsophistication that was hardly a plus. His manners lacked any polish, he appeared to be almost inarticulate, and when he did speak, it was with a pronounced Brooklyn accent. Too bad; not her type.

"No problem," said Tony, trying to be cool. "I'm a friend of Jackie Call's," he added, trying to bridge the obvious gap between them.

Jackie Call? Who the hell was Jackie . . . oh, yes, the little blond chorine. A nobody. Laura began walking to her dressing room, Tony keeping pace with her. "Everybody needs friends," she said noncommittally.

Tony had latched onto his confidence again. "Yeah, I was just sayin' that to somebody this mornin'. Listen, I was wonderin' if maybe we could get together sometime and talk?"

Laura laughed up at him. "About what?" Talk? Was he joking?

It was crowded backstage, and the two of them moved slowly. Dancers, technicians, fans and hangers-on kept calling to Laura from all directions, shouting their congratulations.

"About how incredible you are," Tony told her with all the charm he could muster.

"Thanks again, but I already know."

Caught by surprise, Tony could only ask blankly, "Say what?"

Laura grinned at him provocatively. "I already know," she drawled.

They had reached her dressing room, and Tony

followed her inside. She made no protest. It was a small room, holding a rack of street clothes, a group of costumes hanging in garment bags, a dressing table whose mirror was outlined in theatrical lights. Into the mirror were stuck a number of closing-night telegrams of congratulations. Long-stemmed roses stood in vases, and on the dressing table itself three sprays of dendrobium orchids fluttered like captured butterflies in a black amethyst vase.

As Laura seated herself before the mirror, Tony lounged in the doorway and folded his arms over his chest.

"In case you never heard, in Brooklyn I used to be pretty terrific myself." His confidence was rapidly returning.

Laura laughed but never took her eyes off her own image in the glass. "Used to? What happened?"

"I moved to Manhattan," confessed Tony, laughing with her.

"So what do you do?" the girl asked him without much interest.

"That's a good question."

"Yes, very profound," she drawled.

Tony searched for the words to impress her, to make her tear her eyes away from the mirror and look directly at him.

"Well, what I do is, like, sometimes I see the future like it's already here. An' what I see now is . . . great things are gonna happen to you."

Laura dipped her long fingers into a giant jar of cold cream and smeared it over her heavy theatrical makeup.

"And what great things do you see?"

Tony drew a deep breath. "Well," he said huskily, "I see that tonight you're gonna meet this really nice, y'know, very sensitive type guy who you're probably gonna go very crazy for, once you get to know him and his personality."

Laura bit her lip to keep from smiling. "And where is this sensitive type guy you're talking about?"

"I'll get him," Tony volunteered brightly. He stepped out of the doorway, waited a beat, then popped his head back in, grinning broadly.

Laura stood up; she was smiling. In two long steps she was at the doorway and with one strong movement of her graceful arm she had slammed the door in Tony's face.

It was so unexpected, so violent an action, that Tony stood there for a long minute, entirely rattled. Not only was his pride hurt, but his nose had damn near been broken! He looked around to see if anybody had noticed. Several stagehands were giving him the beady eyeball.

"Strong draft in here," said Tony weakly, meaning the door.

Anger was welling up in him, anger mingled with an even stronger attraction to Laura Ravell. Tony never valued what he could come by easily; he was a man who enjoyed the chase, the battle. It made the eventual surrender even sweeter. This amber-eyed beauty was a challenge, and Tony Manero had never refused a challenge.

He threw open the door of Laura's dressing room with a bang. Laura was sitting at her dressing table, taking the cold cream off her face with a wad of tissues.

"Come in," she invited him sweetly.

Tony was flustered, but managed with a superhuman effort to keep hold of his cool.

"Why did you do that to me?" he asked in a low voice.

"Do what?" Laura sounded innocent.

"Do what?! You almost broke my nose with this door. I'm givin' you some of my best come-ons and you try to mangle my face!" Tony's indignation was genuine.

Laura carefully wiped away the last of the makeup and turned to Tony, smiling. With her face cleaned of the greasepaint she was even more beautiful, her skin pale and translucent.

"I'm sorry about that, but you made a bad mistake," she told him in an even voice. "That being, like most men_you seem to take pleasure in talking to women as though they're stupid."

Tony blinked in surprise. This was something he hadn't expected. "Look," he answered, "if I said something to make ya mad, I apologize. I thought I was bein' sorta charming. And even if you did try to damage my head, see . . . the fact is I still amazingly respect your dancing talent and your womanhood in general. I didn't always respect womanhood, but I've got this new mature outlook going, y'know. I even gave up cursin' and everything. So knowing all this information, I'd like to maybe take you someplace to eat and relax. But it's gotta be informal 'cause all my suits are out being pressed."

He ended his spiel with a broad smile, his large blue eyes twinkling.

Laura suppressed the answering smile that was threatening her lips. "Thanks," she said coolly, "for the apology and the invitation, but I'm going home early tonight. Auditions start for the new show tomorrow."

Tony's ears perked up. "This new show, are you already set for it?"

"Definitely. Are you a dancer?"

"Couldn't you tell?" Tony grinned.

Now Laura did permit herself to smile. "Of course. Listen, why don't you come by the Royale Theater tomorrow? They need thirty dancers. I'll put in a good word for you."

Tony took an instinctive step backward and shook his dark head vehemently. "Don't do that," he said, and he meant it. "You don't have to do that." If there was anything Tony didn't want, it was professional favors. Especially from a woman, despite his "respect for womanhood" rap. And especially from *this* woman. "Can't go out tonight, huh?" he tried one more time.

Laura shook her honey-colored head. "Sorry."

Slowly Tony backed up to the dressing room door.

"Well, I had this commitment anyway. Listen, if I don't see you again, I wanna say it's been really nice being insulted by you."

This time Laura couldn't help smiling. There was something . . . arresting . . . about this uncouth boy. "Aren't you coming to the audition?"

Tony's smile broadened into a dazzling grin. "I *knew* you wanted to see me again," he said triumphantly, and he disappeared out the door.

Laura sat looking after him thoughtfully. Yes, definitely something arresting. Possibilities. Unmannered, uneducated, but real animal magnetism. Her long eyes narrowed as she turned back to her mirror.

Jackie was dressed and ready when Tony picked her up outside the chorus dressing room. She gave him a quizzical look as though asking him silently what had kept him, but she said nothing.

"Ya wanna get something to eat?" Tony asked her as they left the theater by the stage entrance.

"Sure, but won't you be late for work?"

"Don't worry about it," said Tony absently. Then he asked her abruptly, "Did you know they were having auditions at the Royale tomorrow?"

Jackie raised one surprised eyebrow. "I told you that a week ago."

"Maybe I wasn't paying attention," said Tony. He was scowling in thought; his face wore a faraway look that Jackie had rarely seen.

"You're going to try out, aren't you?" she asked him softly.

Tony tried a small smile and an even smaller shrug. "Why not? Rejection is startin' to become a hobby."

It was at this moment that Laura Ravell stepped out of the stage door and walked past them at a rapid pace.

"Small world, isn't it?" she said. "Good night."

"Good night," replied Jackie automatically, assuming that Laura's greeting was for her. But she felt rather than saw Tony stiffen beside her, and when she looked, she could see that Tony's eyes were locked on Laura's receding figure. The penny dropped, and Jackie's green eyes clouded.

" 'Small world'?" she repeated. "Do you know her?"

"Informally," he answered as casually as he could.

"How'd you meet her?"

"I saw her pass by and told her she's an okay dancer." It wasn't exactly a lie, but it wasn't exactly the truth either.

Both of them watched Laura step gracefully into the back seat of a Rolls Royce that had been waiting at the mouth of the alley. Jackie shook her head, marveling.

"You're incredible! You told Laura Ravell she's an okay dancer!"

"Something to that effect."

"I can't believe you said that. She's a *great* dancer! When did she 'pass by'?"

"What about the limo?" Tony was staring hard after the silver Rolls that was trapped in after-theater traffic.

"What about it?" countered Jackie, her mouth in a thin line. She was really hating the turn this conversation was taking. A lump that ached a lot was beginning to form in her belly.

"Whose is it?"

"I don't know. Maybe hers. Everyone says she comes from money."

Whew! Tony's brain was reeling. Beauty, talent and now money too! He had his work cut out for him, and he wasn't even sure yet what "work" he meant. All he knew was that Laura Ravell exerted a mighty pull on his senses and had captured his attention completely.

"Jackie, is this what's her name heavily involved?" He still thought he was being casual.

"Laura?" asked Jackie carefully, with heavy sarcasm.

"Yeah, Laura," said Tony, ignoring the emphasis the girl had placed on the name.

"What do you mean by involved?"

Tony spread out his hands, "Involved. I mean, like have you seen a lot of guys hanging around drooling or something?"

The ache in Jackie's stomach intensified as the lump began to grow. "I just dance and mind my own business," she told him stiffly.

For the first time Tony took a sharp look at Jackie. He could see the anger in her face and he knew that hurt was behind it, but he turned away from Jackie's pain. "Hey, don't get mad 'cause I'm just asking some informal questions," he told her.

His insensitivity made Jackie explode. "Tony, if you're hot over somebody, I don't want to hear about it."

"C'mon," said Tony uneasily, "I just respect her dancin'." Even to his own ears, his words sounded pretty feeble.

"And her legs! And her face!"

Tony decided to bluff it out. "Sure," he said blandly, "I respect all her equipment, because she's got this abundant talent. And I mean, didn't you ever hear how intelligent she speaks?"

This was too much for Jackie. This was the final, the ultimate, the absolute limit of a last straw!

"An accent doesn't make somebody intelligent!" she sputtered. "If it did, you'd be Einstein!" She turned and began to stalk up the street away from Tony, but in two long strides he'd caught up with her.

Laying a mollifying hand on Jackie's arm, he tried to mend his fences. "Wait. Listen, I'm not trying to get you mad, 'cause I think you're a really good dancer."

Jackie shook off his hand and continued to keep her face turned away from him.

"Hey . . . I don't know . . . what can I say. . . ." Tony realized now that Jackie was really angry, really hurt, and it would take more than a little charm turned on to get her to forgive him.

"You wanna go eat or somethin'?"

Jackie stopped and looked straight into Tony's face. "Don't play this game, Tony," she said quietly.

"What game?" But he had a trapped and guilty look behind the assumed innocence of his expression.

Jackie just shook her head sadly. When he was like this, there was no breaking through to him, not to the *real* him. Sometimes she wondered if there *was* a real Tony Manero under all the thick layers of so-called charm. "I'll see you tomorrow," she said quietly.

Tony could ignore Jackie's anger, pretend that the pain wasn't there, but this quiet, resigned attitude really got to him. This he couldn't fight, this he couldn't charm, this he couldn't cajole.

"Look, what're you saying?" He gave it a last shot. "I don't even *know* her."

Jackie uttered one long sigh of exasperation. "Tony, you do what you have to do, just don't lead me on." Then she turned with finality and walked away from him swiftly.

He knew better than to follow. Even so he made one last futile attempt at appeasement. "Lead what on?" he hollered after her. "Hey, Jackie, you were really good tonight. Excellent." As he spoke the words, he realized that they should have been the first ones he'd said, not the last.

Boy, he'd really messed that up! But he could patch things with Jackie; just give him a little time, and she'd be eating out of his hand again. Besides, he really liked her.

But Laura now. Laura was different. Different from anybody he'd ever met, ever even laid eyes on. The memory of her sinuous body on the stage, the skill and art of her dancing, the incredible honey-colored eyes that matched her deep amber hair . . . he couldn't get Laura off his mind.

She had . . . something. Class, maybe? Sure, but Jackie had class. No, it was something else, something that to Tony was indefinable. An attitude, an independence, a ferocity and an arrogance that matched his own. This one would not come easy. Every woman in Tony's life so far had come to him easy, almost begging for his attention and his loving. Not Laura Ravell. She was interested, her curiosity was piqued, Tony could swear to that. But easy, no. Laura Ravell was one big beautiful question mark.

But there was something more. He wanted to dance with her. He wanted to match his body with hers, to hold her in his arms and make her turn, sway, bend, move with him. He wanted to lead her, command her, make his body the dominating one in the dance.

Tomorrow. The auditions were tomorrow. She'd invited him with a curl of her lips and a lift of her lovely brows.

And he'd be there.

Chapter Six

IT WAS IMPRESSIVE. TONY HAD NO IDEA how big, how important this show *Inferno* was going to be until he turned up for the audition. Even for the first cut, the preliminary testing, there were dancers auditioning whom Tony recognized from his rare and expensive visits to the Broadway theater. This was no amateur night in Dixie. This was the big time. This was also the first audition he'd attended where men and women dancers were in the theater together for the first cut. Almost always they auditioned separately at different times of the day until the lucky finalists were brought together to be paired for looks, heights and dancing styles. Tony spotted Jackie in the crowd of women and sent her a silent "good luck."

In the standard audition for dancers, they are asked to perform a "combination" of steps and turns that lasts usually for sixteen bars of music, or roughly two minutes. The choreographer or the assistant choreographer demonstrates what he or she wants, customarily two or three times. Any more than that and they are dealing with slow learners, and nobody wants retards in a show. Okay, let's say three demonstrations, then it's "Show It to Me" time, and you'd better show it, or you're off the stage so fast your tights are smoking.

First you dance the combination as a group a few times to get the steps down correctly and begin to show what you're made of. Then they usually split the group in half, and if the choreographer is patient, they'll split the group again in threes or fours. By this time the "combination" is imprinted on your mind and in your muscles, and you can start exhibiting style. Style is what they're looking for; style is what gets you the job. Style is where all the long years of training and practice and aching muscles and sore feet and rigorous diet and no cigarettes get to pay off, and the irony is you're supposed to make it look easy.

The first cut is the big elimination; if you make it past that, they bring you back to learn another combination. This time they're checking you out for looks as well as style and to see how well you'll fit in with the rest of the dancers. Sometimes they want homogeneity in the chorus line, and they go for boys and girls who look alike, all the same size. In some shows—take *Cats* for example—they want everybody to look different from everybody else, to have a distinctive style and personality all one's own. There is maybe one good job out there for every two hundred and fifty professional dancers, so you can imagine that each audition is crisis time, each rejection can be a matter of surviving or not surviving. God only knows why anybody wants to go through this living hell, this torture, to spend a couple of hours every night—and two matinees a week—dancing his or her heart out up there on a stage.

But thank heaven that dancers *do* go through it. And inside the heart of every boy and girl trying out for even the smallest part is the hope and maybe even the conviction that someday he or she will be a star, break out of the chorus and take center stage. That makes everything worthwhile—all the agony and the poverty and the humiliation and the hard work and the sweat and the rejections. Oh, to be a star!

But this audition was different from most others, and the difference was a man named Jesse Benton. Jesse Benton, a director and choreographer so legendary that he personally had changed the style of show dancing, making it less peppy and preppy, but far more jazzy and sensual. Jesse Benton, tall, strong and very masculine—especially for a choreographer—whose triumphs with women were as legendary as his dancing style. Jesse Benton, whose name on a show was almost a guarantee of a hit.

Benton's auditions were different from most other choreographers' because Jesse Benton was a man who knew exactly what he wanted out of a dancer and whose eye was sharp enough, whose sense of dance keen enough, to spot it right away. His auditions were fast; he showed you the steps twice and that was it. If you couldn't keep up after two demos, you didn't belong on Broadway. He was brusque, he was arrogant, he was opinionated, but no dancer could say with any justification that Jesse Benton was unfair or unkind. When he rejected you, he didn't go out of his way to humiliate you. It was strictly business, call us again sometime.

All of this went through Tony's mind as he stood in the wings of the Royale Theater watching the women dancers go through their paces. It was impressive. The professionalism was impressive, and the man Benton was himself impressive—handsome, bearded, dark and possessed of a pair of fierce intelligent eyes under heavy black brows. Tony felt the blood running more quickly through his veins, although the palms of his hands as usual were like ice. He was always nervous before an audition—there's no performer who isn't—but this time there was even more apprehension tap dancing on his spine.

For one thing, Tony felt closer to the big time than he ever had before. And then too there was Laura. She was already signed for this show, and he wanted to impress her, to show her that he was not merely a kid from Brooklyn with a big mouth, but a dancer to be reckoned with.

The music was coming to a climax, and the girls were making their final spin-turns and semisplits, and . . . it was over! The dancers stood trembling with exhaustion and apprehension as the great Jesse Benton approached them to make his cut. Behind him trailed his assistant, an attractive young woman with a tight body and short curly hair. The woman's name was Joy, and she intended to become a choreographer every bit as good as Benton; meanwhile she worshipped his very footprints and did all his paperwork, taking a lot of the flak onto her own slender shoulders. She was invaluable.

"Good, very good," called Jesse enthusiastically. "Now it's a matter of who's best for the show."

He came up to the nervous dancers and touched the first girl on the shoulder. She was in. The girl turned pale, then red, and trembled as though she were about to faint. But her face broke into a huge relieved smile; she'd made it.

Jesse passed over two other dancers; Jackie's turn was coming up. Tony said a silent Hail Mary and held his breath. He could see the sweat standing out on Jackie's forehead. Her golden hair was limp, and damp tendrils covered her brows and neck. Tony thought he could see, even at this distance, the anxiety in Jackie's green eyes.

Now Jesse had come up to Jackie, and his hand reached out to tap Jackie lightly as a sign of acceptance.

"You work hard, Jackie," he told her approvingly.

Jackie let her breath out in a gasp of relief and turned to Tony in the wings. He gave her a pair of thumbs up as a signal of congratulation and flashed her his widest grin. She *did* work hard, and she was a damn good dancer. He was proud to know her.

"Okay, that's it!" called Jesse, and the other female dancers slumped in dejection. "Thank you all," he said briskly as the girls filed off the stage. "Next group. Let's go!"

The next group was Tony's, and the men dancers moved to the center of the stage.

"Gentlemen, I'm running behind," Jesse told them without preamble. "So I'm going to have to give you bigger chunks of the combination. Gets tougher every year," he added, not without sympathy. He turned to Joy, who stood clasping her precious clipboard on which she had just taken down the names and addresses of the girls Jesse had chosen.

"Okay, I want to take a look now from the orchestra."

Joy nodded and stepped to one side. Jesse gave the signal to the small orchestra, which was made up of a bass guitarist, electric piano and percussion, producing a big sound. As the music broke out, Jesse danced the combination of steps, a long one—twenty-four bars—twice, showing the dancers exactly what he wanted them to do. His dancing was enormously stylish and graceful, and he made it look very easy, but it wasn't. It wasn't at all; Tony saw with mounting apprehension that it was a difficult and challenging routine, one requiring an enormous amount of concentration. His confidence faltered; for the first time he wondered if he could beat out the competition and doubted it.

The demonstration completed, Jesse took a seat in the audience fifth row center and sat with his arms folded. Joy stepped out in his place.

"I'm Joy," she began.

"I'm Happiness," cracked Tony out of nervousness. "How ya doin'?"

There was always one joker in every pack, thought Joy, but it's *so* tiresome. She threw Tony a weary smile and continued as though he hadn't spoken. "I'm the assistant choreographer. So if there are any questions about the routine, ask now."

Nobody dared to open his mouth; the musicians vamped a little as the dancers took their first position.

Tony stared out into the orchestra where Jesse was sitting. He thought he could make out Laura sitting beside him, but he wasn't positive. There were also two other men, but there were always two other men. These were usually the producers, checking up to see where their money was going. Tony's mouth was dry and his hands were wet; it seemed an eternity before the music actually began.

"Make it happen!" called Jesse Benton from the darkness, and the musicians got down.

As the sounds washed over him, Tony discovered the nervousness leaving his body. His muscles responded at once to the music, and he didn't have to give the routine a second thought. It was in there, in his brains, in his legs, in the way he moved his head. The dance was completely inside him, and all he had to do was express it. All around him on the stage, other male dancers were expressing it too, but Tony was oblivious of them. It was he, he alone, Tony and the music, and he was surprised when the music ended and the dance was over. So soon!

A minute or two elapsed while Jesse conferred with the people sitting near him. Then he called out, "Okay. Forty-two and forty-six, please remain. Everybody else, thank you."

Did I hear him right? He did say forty-six. Tony looked at the number pinned to his T-shirt. Forty-six. He hadn't been cut, at least not for the prelim. He stood rooted to the spot, unable to move or laugh or even think. He'd been chosen. He'd been asked to stay, to dance again. All around him the other dancers were moving offstage glumly, rejected, cut, out of it.

"Well, Happiness, you're off," said Joy briskly to him.

"Off?" replied a dazed Tony. "He said forty-six. I'm forty-six."

Joy checked his number, then her clipboard, then she nodded. "Sorry. So you stay for the next cut." She didn't sound very enthusiastic; she was still thinking of Tony as a loudmouth clown.

Tony gave her a smile of relief. "Ya know, that mistake coulda wrecked destiny." Again he scanned the orchestra floor, searching for Laura, but she was nowhere to be seen. Had it been Laura sitting there after all? Had she watched him dance, seen him chosen?

"Let's go! Look alive!" called Jesse impatiently, and the last of the dancers left the stage as the next audition group came on. Mopping the sweat off his face with the towel from his gym bag, Tony sidled over to Jackie. He hadn't seen her to speak to since their quarrel last night.

He gave her his famous ingratiating grin-with-the-twinkle-in-the-blue-eyes. "In case I fall into the orchestra pit and ya never see me again, I want ya to know that I think you've got exceptional legs."

Jackie glanced down at her abbreviated audition leotard which did, indeed, show off her long legs. She couldn't help smiling back. "So do you," she said approvingly, with a saucy eye on Tony's tights.

Knowing that she wasn't angry with him anymore made Tony feel immeasurably better, and they stood side by side as friends, watching the last of the dancers audition.

It was time for the second cut, and the butterflies in Tony's stomach came back, this time dressed as tigers. Joy was there with the clipboard, but Jesse too was on the stage. He wanted to see this part of the audition from closer range. This was the crucial one.

"Okay, first positions," Joy called and made herself scarce. Now it was only Jesse and the dancers with no go-betweens.

All eyes were on Jesse Benton, whose face wore an expression of intense purpose.

"Listen up, this time I want something different. Do the whole combination through once more, and at the end I want you to use the basic movements of the sequence to improvise. I want to see you extend the style until it becomes your natural style. All right. Get ready."

If you needed one word to describe the expression on twelve male dancers' faces, that word could only be *stunned*. Jesse had taken them all by surprise and thrown them into consternation. This was more than they'd bargained for, more than any choreographer had ever asked them to do at an audition. Tony, who had rarely survived the first audition cut and who had never yet danced in a show, felt a cold chill of fear. Was this where he'd go down the drain? He snuck a look at Jackie standing in the wings; the girl gave him an encouraging nod and blew a little silent kiss for good luck. He found himself looking again for Laura in the audience. Was that her sitting there? He couldn't be certain.

Now the music began again, and a dozen dancers broke into the one long routine which by now was second nature to them. Tony too found it easier this time. Having performed those steps, he could duplicate them almost without thinking, the tempo of the music providing an automatic impetus.

Now Jesse's voice was raised above the music.

"Good! Now keep it going! Improvise. It's *your* time, let it go! Let it happen. Take it anywhere. *Do* it!"

The musicians picked up the tempo a little, the bass laying down a strong melodic line and the drums picking up the beat. Eleven bodies began to move, independent of each other, no longer a group of dancers.

Eleven bodies began to move, and Tony Manero just stood there for what seemed to be a year. Actually it was no more than twenty seconds, but you wouldn't want to sit on a hot stove until the count of twenty was completed. Then he began to move, slowly, diffidently, as if looking for something.

Whatever he was looking for, it took him a minute to find it, and he found it inside himself, not outside.

The music took him over and entered into his bones. It was as if some inner voice were talking to him, encouraging him, telling him what to do. His concentration was total.

His movements became surer, broader and more exciting. He turned, his arms held up, and his body was one tall streak of dancing lightning. Ignoring the dancers around him, Tony began to move freely around the stage with the grace of a prowling jungle cat, improvising. His muscles stood out strongly under the tight-fitting dance clothes, and he appeared to be carved of marble, black for the clothing, white marble for the body beneath it, a Michelangelo sculpture come to life. He was breathtaking. Jackie, standing in the wings, felt the hair on the nape of her neck rising as she watched him. Tony seemed to be the embodiment of freedom itself, freedom dancing.

I've never seen him move like that, she thought.

Jesse raised his arm to call a halt, and the music stopped suddenly. They had been dancing less than two minutes, but to Tony it seemed a lifetime.

"Good! Very good!" said Jesse. "We'll take your résumés or names and numbers and get back to you in twenty-four hours. We'll only be selecting two men. If you're not one of them, I want you to know you were excellent."

Two men! Twenty-four hours! Tony was in shock. The adrenaline pumping through his veins came to an abrupt halt, leaving him drained. This couldn't happen to him! They *had* to pick him, *had* to! His life depended on it! Never had he felt this way, this strongly about an audition. Now he felt as though a rug had been yanked out from under him, sending him tumbling head over heels into space. He tried to catch his breath, but couldn't, and it came from his throat in ragged gasps.

Suddenly, Laura's face. The face he'd been searching for. Laura was standing in the wings watching him. And she was smiling. She was wearing rehearsal clothes, her legs impossibly beautiful in the high-cut leotard. And smiling at him, at Tony Manero.

Almost in a daze he walked over to her, feeling the sweat from his exertions trickling down the sides of his tight-fitting shirt, feeling the sweat drying on his shoulders and on his cheeks.

"I know what you're thinking," she told him in that low, seductive drawl of hers.

"Do you?" Tony panted.

"They'll call," she said with confidence, adding, "You're not bad."

This he took as a compliment, although not a very big compliment. "Thanks," he said wryly.

But Laura was smiling again, nodding her beautiful head. "I mean it."

Tony saw his opening and took it. "Ah, listen, can I ask you a favor?"

That lovely chin tilted up at him, and the sleek brow, so expressive, was raised. "What?" asked Laura.

His blue eyes gleamed in his handsome face as he looked down at her. "If I appreciate you, and it looks like maybe you appreciate me, what do you think about maybe spendin' some time appreciating each other?"

His confidence had returned because Laura had seen him dance. He was good, he knew it, and now she knew it too. He might be some bigmouth kid from Brooklyn, granted, but he was a bigmouth kid with talent. And that made all the difference in the world.

"Appreciating?" purred Laura, as though she were tasting the word.

"For many hours," grinned Tony.

She gave him the old double-o, the once-over, looking him up and down as though she were pricing him by the pound. What a woman! Tony just stood there, basking in her gaze, because he knew he could pass any visual test. His body was a magnificent instrument, tall, strong, muscular and disciplined. And the cleft in his chin didn't hurt either.

Laura looked at Tony long and hard while she considered her answer. No doubt about it, he was one magnificent animal, and a very tempting prospect. Of course she had to consider their relative positions. She was a lead dancer, star of an upcoming Broadway show, and he, if he got lucky, would be a chorus boy. Still she couldn't deny that she was attracted to him, very attracted. Tony possessed a masculine magnetism that was very powerful, almost overwhelming. And he was coming on very strong.

But what had moved her most was watching him dance. Whatever "it" was that set certain performers apart from others, he had it. That mysterious something, talent, drive, call it what you will, Tony Manero had it in full measure, and Laura recognized that. Yes, he was very tempting. . . .

"I have a singing lesson that I'll have to cancel," she told him flirtatiously.

"Yeah," said Tony. "I'll have to cancel my dance class."

"I'll have to cancel my manicure," she continued.

"I'll cancel my meeting with the mayor," Tony responded, deadpan.

"Then I'll have to cancel my yoga class."

"I'll cancel my brain operation."

"Don't cancel that!" Laura broke up, and Tony's laughter joined hers. It was the first laughter they had shared, and it signaled Laura's unspoken agreement to "appreciate." For many hours.

Chapter Seven

PARIS IS BEAUTIFUL IN THE SPRING; TAORmina is perfection in the winter; Aspen, Colorado makes the summer memorable; and every part of Switzerland is lustrous in the fall. But for two young people on their first date, nothing on the face of the earth beats New York City. Dirty, noisy, crowded, dangerous, it's still the most exciting place you can think of. It's the glory of Greece and the grandeur of Rome and the temples of Angkor Wat and the great pyramid of Egypt all rolled into one. And a lot of it is free.

Walking is free, the zoo is free, Fifth Avenue is free, the art museums are free on Tuesday, people-watching is free, Chinatown is free, the SoHo galleries are free, window-shopping is free.

Eating and drinking are of course expensive.

On one of those very crisp mid-December days filled with the promise of snow on the bare trees, when even New York City smells fresh and fine, Tony and Laura changed out of their dance clothes and went out into the city to spend time together and learn about each other. And New York, seeing two tall, beautiful young

people, opened up and said "welcome." Even the
Santa Clauses rang their bells harder when they saw
these two.

It was a day to make even a mugger smile. On Fifth
Avenue the bagpipe player was out, dressed in all his
Scottish regalia, playing laments on the pipes, while
delighted passersby dropped quarters and dimes and
even dollar bills into his bagpipe case. Outside the
Museum of Modern Art, a mime, his face painted
white and his dark clothes making his skinny body all
but invisible, acted out *The Wall*. A string quartet of
Juilliard music students sat in front of Saks Fifth
Avenue playing Bartók. They were all making bo-
nanza bucks off the Christmas shoppers. On such a
day as this, Romeo deserted Rosaline in favor of
Juliet. On such a day as this, Tony deserted Jackie in
favor of Laura.

He told her everything about himself, making her
laugh. He painted a picture of Bay Ridge as a mighty
duchy with himself as duke, though both of them knew
he was exaggerating. Gesturing with his long expressive fingers, he told her his hopes and his dreams, his
determination to succeed, his physical need to dance.
He told her as much as he could, hoping to impress
her.

She, on the other hand, told him practically nothing
about herself, yet Tony hardly noticed, because her
soft, drawling voice was musical in his ears saying
even the little she said. And she was a good listener.

Tony couldn't take his eyes off Laura. Her body
moved with such supple grace that even walking, she
looked as though she were dancing. Her long tousled
hair gleamed in the thin winter sunlight, and her lovely
skin glowed. So many men turned to look at her, to
become enraptured at the sight of her, that Tony was
torn between jealousy and pride. Pride won out.

Never had Tony been with a woman as beautiful as
Laura Ravell. And she seemed to him so totally together, moving with confidence through life as though

she had it knocked. And why not? Wasn't everything sitting in the palm of her lovely hand? Although Tony couldn't discount the many long years she must have worked to become the dancer she was, she made it look so effortless that even he, who could count every drop of sweat he'd shed for his art, thought she must have had it easy.

The short winter day passed quickly, too quickly, punctuated by their laughter and their pleasure in each other's company. And suddenly it was evening and Laura was ravenous, clamoring to be fed. Tony's belly had already been crying "Pizza! Chinese food!" for hours, but he'd been unsure about mentioning food to her, afraid she'd remember a dinner date somewhere else and go off and leave him.

They were in SoHo, surrounded by fancy charcuteries and nouvelle cuisine restaurants where the emphasis was on small portions and big hanging plants. But they were only a ten-minute walk from Little Italy with its steaming plates of pasta and tomato sauce and the crisp goodness of fried squid. Umberto's or Bertino's and maybe Ferrara's for dessert, with gobs of sweetened ricotta cheese oozing out of the crisp cannoli. Tony was drooling already.

"Sushi," said Laura firmly.

"Sure," agreed Tony. What the hell was sushi?

Sushi, he found to his horror, was raw fish wrapped around rice balls, inside which lurked a green horseradish mustard so hot it dissolved your teeth. Not only was sushi raw fish, but you had to squat barefoot on straw mats and eat it with wooden chopsticks. Insult to injury! It wasn't cheap either, and Tony gasped when he saw the right side of the menu with the prices.

But the Duke of Bay Ridge was nothing if not cool, and Tony Manero succeeded in choking down sushi without bringing it back up. He even managed to get a good laugh out of Laura "pretending" that he couldn't use chopsticks, and he ended up spearing the slimy stuff, like harpooning a miniature whale.

Laura of course could manipulate chopsticks as though born with a silver pair in her mitt and managed to wolf down two plates of raw fish with the delicacy of an empress handling the crown jewels.

Thank God Tony could recognize the dessert; it was honeydew melon.

As they sipped their tea, Tony began to relax. The grisly part of the meal was over. He looked across the table at Laura, almost unable to believe his good fortune. Would he dare to put the moves on her, this woman he'd been waiting for all his twenty-four years? As though daring himself to do it, he pushed his shoeless foot across to hers and touched her ankle ever so delicately with his toes.

Coolly, without looking up from her teacup, Laura moved her foot away. Still the question mark, the beautiful question mark. He waited a beat, then once more he moved his foot toward hers . . . an inch away . . . a half inch . . . now the toes lightly grazed the ankle.

This time Laura's foot didn't move.

Tony held his breath while his blue eyes sought her amber ones. She looked back boldly, deeply into his eyes.

Tony moved his foot closer to Laura's until their ankles were touching. Setting down her teacup, Laura looked him full in the face. There was a questing look in her eyes, provocative, tantalizing.

Then, with great deliberation, Laura's foot moved away. Before Tony could register his disappointment, he felt a touch on his leg. Her toes were moving ever so slowly up his leg, leaving a little trail of fire on Tony's skin. It was the most erotic moment of his life, and yet it was nothing more than a foot and a leg. No, it was everything more. It was the hint of the exploration to come, of tingling touches.

I'm gonna melt, Tony thought. *I'm gonna melt right into this stupid straw mat. This is the sexiest woman in the world. God give me strength.*

But it wasn't time for that yet. Laura wanted to go dancing. This was as exciting for Tony; he wanted to dance with Laura, ached for it. And because it was his night off, and he was with the sexiest woman in the world, he took her to The Savage Instinct to show her off to Fred and Barry and everybody on the dance floor who had ever seen him washing glasses and serving drinks.

And show her off he did. The music was hot, but Tony and Laura were hotter; they burned up the floor together. Both of them were conscious of the chemistry between them and of how good they looked as a couple. Their movements became more and more sensual, responding to the music, to the colored lights, but most especially to each other's bodies. It was what Tony had been waiting for, it was the only way in which he was able to dominate and lead Laura, through the dance. Dancing with her, he was totally the male and she the elusive female, now teasing, now submissive, now demure. Their dance was pure fire, and Tony gloried in the envious glances of the others. They were the center of attention, and they deserved to be.

And then at last it was their time alone together.

A doorman building on Seventy-third Street and Park Avenue is hardly what a featured dancer who has only just been cast as a lead can afford, unless she shares it with five other dancers. But Laura Ravell shared this space only with art, with abstract paintings lit by tiny bronze lamps and strange sculptures on pedestals of marble. The space itself was unbelievable—rooms as large as football fields with views of Central Park and the lights of downtown Manhattan. Large, deep sofas covered in dove gray velvet flanked a marble fireplace. The floors of the apartment's foyer were marble too, and the walls were covered in matching gray suede. Even the bathroom was marble where it wasn't mirrored, and the tub had eight whirlpool jets.

The apartment was on the twentieth floor, and french doors led from the living room out onto a balcony large enough to hold metal chairs and a table, a chaise longue of steel mesh and several potted trees. Barefoot and dressed only in his jeans, Tony stepped out on the balcony. Bewildered, he tried to drink it all in but failed.

"Laura, what is all this?" he asked as he turned from the balcony to see her approaching. "I never seen anything like this. You born rich or something?"

Laura shook her head playfully and smiled, but there was a warning undercurrent in her voice. "I told you before, don't ask."

"What is it? Some big secret?"

She shrugged. "It's just furniture," she said, not masking a tinge of contempt in her words.

But Tony was still struggling to understand. This was important to him, to *them,* couldn't she see that?

"A dancer would have to work ten shows at the same time to live here."

"We had a good night," said Laura.

"Wait a minute. Did I miss something here?"

Laura traced her finger thoughtfully around one of Tony's pectoral muscles and trailed it over his bicep.

"I changed the subject," she told him coolly. "We had a good time."

"Yeah, we did." He definitely had to admit that. The best time ever, a night to go down in history. Tired as he was, he wanted this night never to end.

"Listen, Laura, I want to tell you something, and I don't want you to take it the wrong way," he began, his arm around her slender shoulders.

"What?"

His arm tightened around her.

"Y'know, I haven't met many people I respect. But you really did something with your life, and I just wanna say that I really think you're significant."

"Thank you," said Laura quietly, but Tony felt her body resisting him ever so slightly.

Tony Manero

Jackie Call

Laura Ravell

Auditioning for the chorus of *Satan's Alley*

Rehearsal break

Tony reaches a turning point.

Rehearsing

Tony and Laura have it out.

Laura arrives for opening night.

Finale

"When you dance, it's like watchin' smoke move."

"Is it?" Laura suddenly didn't sound all that thrilled.

"Yeah," said Tony enthusiastically, giving her shoulder a squeeze and a nudge. "I could watch you for hours."

Neither the squeeze nor the nudge evoked a response from the shoulder. Instead Laura said almost distantly, "You can't dance forever, can you?"

"No," agreed Tony. "But ya always know ya have that talent in you, and that never leaves. Right?"

But Laura was turning her face away from his as he bent to kiss her.

"I think maybe . . . well, I think it's time to say good night."

"Something wrong?"

"It's three o'clock," Laura pointed out.

A grin broke over Tony's handsome face. "No problem. I take vitamins," he bragged.

Laura slipped deftly out from under his encircling arm. "I have to work on a routine early tomorrow," she said firmly.

It sunk in at last, but Tony had a hard time believing it. "Y'know, this is a flash. I've never been asked to leave before." His eyes shadowed to dark blue as his broad smile faded.

Laura shrugged lightly. "Don't take it personally."

"I have to. I'm the only other person here," replied Tony with some stiffness. He fought to hang onto his cool, but he was hurting and surprised at just how much he was hurting. He waited a beat, and when Laura seemed to have nothing more to say, he added, "Then I should definitely leave." It was half a question, half a statement.

Laura nodded. "I think so."

Drawing a deep breath, Tony asked, "Is this it? I mean, like tonight it's over?"

She shook her lovely head and moved closer to him,

touching him one last time. "Just until tomorrow," she half whispered. It sounded like a promise.

With the half promise still echoing in his ears, Tony was out of there in four minutes. The night air was cold, much colder than the day had been. He shivered in his light leather jacket and turned the collar up over his neck and ears. An icy wind was blowing across Park Avenue; people without money could catch pneumonia on this street, 'cause only the rich were riding around in big warm cars.

Tony turned west, toward the park, his footsteps sounding loud in the deserted darkness. Over and over he thought about the events of the day and the evening, trying to sort them out so that they made sense.

They'd had a great time, a fantastic time. He knew that *he* had, and he didn't think Laura was a good enough actress to fake her good time. Besides, why should she? The day had been everything two people could want, a drawing together, a matching. The evening had been great too. Dancing like that, as if they'd been born to dance together, all eyes watching them, envying them. What a trip! He was certain that she'd gotten as big a kick out of it as he had.

Even the yucky raw fish had been fun in its own way, although it would be a very cold day in hell before Tony Manero would go for sushi again.

So why was he freezing his tail off on a windy street at three A.M., instead of cuddling next to that great-looking lady on those ruffled sheets in that king-size bed in that Hollywood movie set of an apartment? It wasn't natural.

And that apartment, mystery number two and Excedrin headache number one hundred and fourteen. Where did she get the bread to live in Buckingham Palace? Tony had no idea of the dollar value of the art and the furnishings in Laura's place—those ruffled sheets alone had cost six hundred dollars at Pratesi, and that was without the pillow cases or the comforter—but even a boy from Bay Ridge could smell luxury when it was shoved under his nose. All that marble and suede and velvet didn't come cheap. Not on Park Avenue. He knew what he had to pay a month for his fleabag, and what Jackie paid for a cramped little West Side apartment; that Park Avenue pad was probably a condo, and the maintenance alone must be twenty times what he and Jackie paid put together.

Jackie. Suddenly Tony was very lonely for Jackie. She was really his best friend, maybe the only true friend he had in the world. He wanted to go to her and tell her about Laura, ask for her advice, what she thought about it. Was it going to be a relationship or what? But it wasn't cool to talk to Jackie about Laura. Uncomfortably Tony recognized something of her feelings for him; they went way beyond friendship and were grounded in their old love affair. He couldn't tell Jackie, he shouldn't even mention Laura's name to her.

Now he was lonelier than ever, and he still couldn't help thinking about Jackie. She'd be asleep now, all soft and warm and snuggly under the covers with her little nose wrinkled like it did when she slept. Asleep, she looked like a child; her short blond hair would tousle up into cute cowlicks. Jackie would never put him out the door at three in the morning as though he were some stray alley cat.

He was passing a phone booth now, one of the few that worked. Impulsively he stepped inside and reached into his pocket. A dime. Murphy's Law was inoperative tonight. Thinking of cuddling next to the warmth of Jackie, he dialed her number. A ring. Two. Three. He swore under his breath. Wasn't she home?

Jackie picked up the phone on the third ring, and her voice was cross and sleepy. "Hello?"

"Hi, babe, it's me."

"Tony? Is that you, Tony? What time is it? Where are you? What are you doing?"

Tony kept his voice light. "Patrolling the city. Making the streets safe for women and children. Somebody's gotta do it."

"Are you okay?" Jackie sounded entirely bewildered.

"Great. Listen, are you alone?"

"What?" She didn't understand the question, sleepiness still fogging her brain.

"Are you alone?" repeated Tony. "I mean, like is there a vacancy next to you?" For some reason, he was anxious about her reply.

"There's a vacancy," said Jackie, beginning to wake up. "Why?" she added rather coyly.

As soon as she'd answered, Tony changed his mind. He wasn't sure why, but all of a sudden he didn't want to go over there and crawl into that warm bed next to Jackie. Maybe it was conscience, maybe a flicker of sensitivity, maybe he simply thought it was unfair to take his loneliness and his anxieties out on Jackie, to use her without her consent.

Or maybe he just simply changed his mind.

Anyway, all he said was, "Just curious. Listen, you shouldn't be on the phone so late. A professional needs to watch her health. See ya tomorrow." He hung up quickly, leaving a very puzzled Jackie to stare into the darkness a long time before going back to sleep.

Now he felt more tired and depressed than ever. He looked back over his shoulder at Park Avenue, seeing Laura's apartment building looming tall, imposing and unapproachable, only a few lights showing. Then he began to run across the park transverse, anxious to be home, as uninviting as "home" was. He needed sleep. A professional needs to watch his health, wasn't that what he'd just told Jackie?

Besides, he was expecting a telephone call, or if not

expecting, at least hoping for one. And within twenty-four hours. That's what Jesse Benton had said.

"We'll get back to you in twenty-four hours. We'll only be selecting two men."

Two men. Would he be one of them? Tomorrow he'd know.

Chapter Eight

New Yorkers in general and aspiring professionals in particular are linked umbilically to the telephone. The day the phone circuits went out in lower Manhattan thanks to a fire in one of the switching centers downtown, and there was no telephone service for a week, two actors and a nightclub comic killed themselves out of desperation.

Every would-be actor, dancer, singer, comedian, window or set dresser, flower arranger or street peddler has a service. "Call my service," they'll tell you. "This is my service number." An answering service is something they just can't do without. Con Edison may shut off the gas; they may not have enough dimes for the clothes dryer in the laundromat; they may not have tasted real food since the last time they went home to mother, but they all have a service.

Tony of course had told Joy to "call my service," and had given her a telephone number. The grungy single-room-occupancy hotel where he was sacking out had something that had once functioned as a switchboard, and an ancient and decrepit unshaven relic who had once furnished as a doorman-cum-desk clerk sat behind it. But he never took messages, or if he did, he never passed any along to Tony, and under no circumstances could he be described as a service.

Tony of course did not have a service. The number he had given Joy was that of the public telephone mounted on the wall at the end of a long hallway outside his room. If he left the door slightly ajar, Tony could hear the phone ring and leap on it. Which was what he intended to do, even if it took every minute of the next twenty-four hours. One does not go to sleep in New York City with one's door slightly ajar, but Tony would rather have had his throat cut than miss hearing the phone ring. Fortunately the guy who'd lived on his floor until he'd been found stiff in an alley, the one who used to run numbers, had gone to his just reward a couple of months earlier, and the phone at the end of the hallway outside Tony's door which used to ring every two minutes now rang infrequently. Otherwise he'd have been up from three-thirty A.M., which was when he'd got home, until eight-thirty A.M., which it was now, just grabbing the phone for the numbers runner.

It was the eight-thirty phone call that wakened Tony from a groggy sleep. With one bound, he exploded out of bed and ran down the corridor in his underwear. He got the phone on the fifth ring.

"Yeah," he said breathlessly into the receiver. "Hello! Tony Manero speaking. Who? No, there's nobody here by that name. I'm here, nobody else. And listen, this phone is out of order for twenty-four hours, hear? So for twenty-four hours, don't call. That's right, don't call. Who, me? I'm a cop. That's right, a cop!"

Furious and disappointed, he slammed down the receiver, glaring at the mangy and elderly tenant whose head poked out of his room door.

"Somebody ought to slam your head, not the phone," crabbed Tony's neighbor.

"Say what? Why don't you try it?" Belligerent and

morose, he wandered down the dusty corridor back to his room, his bare toes catching in the frayed edges of the ragged holes in the hallway carpet.

Great! All he had to do for the next twenty-four hours was to guard the hall phone like a dragon and keep everybody in the crummy joint from using it. *Plus* he had to answer it for every twinkie getting an incoming call. *WON*derful. It was slow death, the worst kind of waiting of all, waiting to hear if you got the job.

Throwing himself back onto his bed, Tony stared up at the ceiling, his eyes following the cracks as his thoughts fell crushingly in on him. The euphoria of last night, of the evening spent with Laura, had all dissipated, leaving him feeling sorry for himself. He'd been working his butt to the bone for years, and he couldn't even afford an answering service! What kind of professional was he? Here he was living in this one-room flypaper, instead of at least a decent studio apartment. Nostalgic thoughts of Bay Ridge crowded his brain. His own room, neat as a new pin. His own posters on the wall—Bruce Lee and Rocky and the fantastical Farrah Fawcett. His own crucifix, lovingly hung there by his mother's reverent hands, the cross usually holding a piece of palm from last year's Palm Sunday Mass for good luck.

His own beautiful clothes, hung in his own closet, not hanging from nails in the wall like here. Shoes all neatly arranged on the closet floor with trees in them to keep their shape. Everybody knew that Tony Manero was the hottest dresser in Bay Ridge, maybe even in all of Brooklyn.

And his laundry, done for him by his mother, no starch in the collars and all the shirts pressed by hand and hung on hangers, just the way he liked them. All the hangers facing in the same direction; Tony had been very picky about that. Here he washed out what he could in the sink, and his laundry dripped all over his tiny room on makeshift clotheslines he'd strung himself. Tony sighed; you never knew when you had it good until you didn't have it anymore. Or as Jackie from Omaha would say, you never miss the water 'til the well runs dry.

Tony was starving now, but he couldn't leave his post by the telephone. Why hadn't he thought to stop at an all-night deli and pick up a six-pack and some taco chips at least? Maybe even some of that pepperoni in the plastic and a hunk of cheese. Maybe his mother *had* scorched the dinner at least once a week, but her food was nourishing and filling. He could smell it scorching now . . .

Damn! He *was* smelling something scorching! He jerked upright in bed and nearly dislocated his spine; then he saw what had happened and uttered a howl of rage mingled with despair.

Last night he'd come in so late and so tired that he'd pulled his shoes off and tossed them aside, instead of standing them neatly together under the bed as he usually did. One of them had fallen under the radiator, and the steam had come on full during the night, the leaky valve scorching the leather and actually shrinking the shoe.

Tony almost wept. Good clothes were one of his passions, especially shoes, and he couldn't afford them anymore. These were his best ones, and practically new. *Were* was the operative word here; the shoe was ruined, and unless he was lucky enough to lose a leg, he'd never wear this pair again. And with his luck, he'd lose the *other* leg!

Bitterly he turned to the radiator and snarled at it as though it were a malevolent person.

"Ya had to do it, didn't ya? Had to wreck my shoes! There goes my transportation!" He glared up at the cracked ceiling and beyond it to Heaven itself. "I'm payin' my dues here!" he told God. "C'mon, gimme a break, here! Go pick on Russia! Please?"

At that instant like a cue from Heaven itself, there was a crash outside Tony's window. He lunged and opened it.

His window sill was the only refrigerator he had; a small container of yogurt and a little bottle of orange juice stayed cold there in the winter air. Somebody had thrown a bag of trash out of a window above, and it had landed on Tony's sill, spilling the yogurt and breaking the orange juice bottle. As he stared in disbelief, another piece of trash, a heavy liquor bottle, whizzed past his ears, missing his head by no more than two inches.

"You're pigs up there, ya know that? Pigs!" roared Tony, but in vain. There was nobody there. It was as though the garbage had thrown itself, which in New York would not be too surprising.

Terrific. It was going to be *some* day. Maybe he should never have left Bay Ridge. What had it gotten him so far? A lot of hard work, a lot of grief.

Introspection was not Tony's long suit, but then neither was inaction. It irked him mightily to be stuck like this minding the phone, never mind the anxiety every time it rang . . .

Never mind the anxiety when it *didn't* ring. For the millionth time, it occurred to him that maybe the phone wouldn't be ringing for him today. Maybe it would be ringing for two other guys. Two out of twelve, and neither one of them him. What would he do in that case? He'd survive, he'd have no other choice. But what would it mean? That he'd never work in a Broadway show? That no choreographer would ever take a chance on him, no director ever pick him for the job? Maybe he wasn't right for the theater. For discos, yes, but maybe not for Broadway.

Doubts and anxieties assailed him, sapping Tony's confidence. He wouldn't be called; he'd never get to dance with Laura; maybe even she wouldn't want to see him again. A one-night stand, that's who he was. What had Cathy said the other night at The Savage

Instinct? "Guys like you are exercise!" The words had been sour grapes then, but they came back now to burn into him, searing his thoughts.

He looked at his watch; it was close to noon, and no call yet. He was going antsy in this tiny room, prowling the dusty corridor like a caged panther, glaring at the phone, hating it, loving it, begging it. He'd never begged for anything in his life before, but now he was whispering to an inanimate telephone, cajoling it, sweet-talking it, pleading with it.

"Ring . . . please, please ring. Ring, c'mon. Ring."

Anytime he even suspected that another tenant was trying to make a call, Tony would bolt out of his room, tear down the corridor, grab the receiver off the hook and pretend to be talking himself, and all the while his finger would be pressing the hook down so that the phone could ring if it wanted to. *Nobody* was going to get to that pay phone today except over Tony Manero's prone body.

Suddenly he felt an impulse to talk to his mother. He hadn't spoken to her in a very long time, and guilt ate at him. It was all those Brooklyn memories; he hardly ever gave his mother a thought these days. Maybe it was natural for a young man his age who'd left home to forget to call his mom, but Mrs. Manero had been going through a lot in the last few years, and he really ought to give her an occasional break.

The nest was empty. The Manero house, which had been noisy and crowded with life, was silent and hollow now, and the seven rooms were too many for Tony's mother. First Tony's brother, Frank, had left the priesthood, a heavy blow for Mrs. Manero to bear, and then he'd gone off to work at a settlement house in Harrisburg, Pennsylvania. Next old Mrs. Santini, Tony's grandmother, who couldn't speak a word of English, had passed on quietly in the night. Soon after, Tony had crossed the bridge into Manhattan. And once little Rosalie had grown up and gone off to college, Tony's father had done a really amazing thing. He'd

left Tony's mother. Italian men didn't do that, but
Luigi Manero had. One day he'd simply packed up and
left. It turned out that he'd had a woman somewhere
for years on the side, and now that the kids had gone,
so had he. He went to live with his "chippie," as Mrs.
Manero called her bitterly.

And you know what the funny thing was? The other
woman was no young blond, no cheap trick, but a
serious middle-aged Italian widow who looked, acted
and sounded very much like Tony's mother. Go figure
that!

Every now and then Mr. Manero would send a few
dollars home, but with increasing rarity. He figured
that since the mortgage was paid on the house, and old
Mrs. Santini had left behind a few bucks in the hole cut
in her mattress, his responsibilities were over. Let
Rosalie get a scholarship; girls didn't have to go to
college anyway.

Let the phone ring, Tony bargained with God, *and
I'll call my mother. Please. I promise.*

The phone remained silent. Cold, black, silent.

A quarter to two. A quarter past two. A quarter to
three, there's no one in the place except you and me.
*I'm getting punchy. A little more of this and I'll be
walking upside down on the ceiling.*

The phone rang.

It's not for me, Tony told himself as he galloped
down the hallway. It's not for me. It can't be. Don't be
too disappointed, he warned himself as he grabbed up
the receiver. It's a wrong number. But he nearly pulled
the phone out of the wall in his desperate anxiety.

It wasn't a wrong number. It was for Tony, and it
was Joy, and she was telling him that he had the job
and when to report for rehearsals and what was his
social security number and how much he was going to
be paid and did he have an agent and could he get her
some head shots for publicity and did he have an
Equity card and who to call at Equity to get a tempo-
rary one for rehearsals. And to all of this Tony made

presumably intelligent and comprehensible answers, while all the time his brain was spinning like a catherine wheel in his head.

I got the job! I got the job! I can't believe it! They hired me! I'm in! I got the job!

With a cry of joy that was loud enough to freeze the blood of everybody within earshot, he did an Indian war dance in triumph on his way back to his room.

"Did you do it, or did you do it?" he exulted. "Way to go, Manero!" Clenching his fists he gave the arms-up signal of victory to the world in general and nobody in particular.

Then he froze in his tracks remembering his bargain with God, and raced back to the phone to keep his part.

His mother's joy upon hearing his voice only made him feel guiltier for not having called sooner.

"Hello, Tony? It's about time I hear from you," she bubbled. "You okay? You're not hurt?"

"I'm okay," he told her happily. "I got a job. Broadway!"

"Gotta job on Broadway?" echoed his mother. "Doin' what?"

Even that didn't bother Tony. Right now he was too happy to care. "Dancin'," he answered patiently. "I dance, remember?"

"How much you get paid?"

"Who cares! I gotta job!"

"No nudity, I hope. Keep your clothes on, Tony," she told him for about the hundred and twentieth time this year.

"Yeah, I will," he promised. Then more seriously, "How ya been?"

There was a long, deep sigh at the other end of the phone. "Good. Okay. Not too bad," said Mrs. Manero without conviction.

"Heard from dad?" asked Tony with some hesitation.

"He don't call no more. I don't know where he is."

His mother's voice was bitter, and the sadness of silence fell between them.

"Yeah, listen," said Tony at last, "I gotta go. I'll call ya back later. See ya." He hung up the phone, feeling a sharp pang of loss, of his home, of his childhood, of the old neighborhood, even of his innocence. He had a sudden clear vision of himself in his First Communion suit. It had been white, with a large white satin bow tied around his right arm and a white satin cover on his Bible to match.

Then the overwhelming affirmation that he had a job on Broadway came thundering over him, blotting out all other thoughts, all bittersweet memories.

I got the job!

His next thought was to see Laura.

Chapter Nine

FREED FROM THE TELEPHONE WATCH, Tony was able to shower, shave and dress at leisure. He wanted to share this day of rejoicing with Laura, but he was pretty sure she was going to be busy. After all, hadn't she canceled her singing lesson, manicure and yoga class in order to "appreciate" him yesterday? And she'd probably also be down at the theater, blocking out some of the important scenes with Jesse. She said she had to work on a routine. But later . . .

At least he could give her a call, maybe get her answering machine and leave a message on it. He telephoned Information for her number only to learn to his chagrin that it was an unlisted one, and no amount of charm or cajoling or demanding to speak to the supervisor had gotten Tony the number. He could kick himself for not getting it from Laura! Now that he'd come to think of it, the dials on the designer telephones in her apartment were empty of a number. He'd meant to ask her about that, but they'd been so busy . . .

Tony thought briefly of maybe going down to the

111

Royale, but he dismissed the thought. First of all it wasn't too cool for a newly hired chorus dancer to go chasing after the star where the rest of the company could see. Time enough for the others to learn about their relationship. Second there was a certain amount of professionalism involved in leaving Laura alone during working hours to do her own thing. And in the third place he knew instinctively that with Laura it wouldn't pay to look too eager. So what he'd do is this: he'd dress, and maybe he'd go crosstown to her apartment building and see if she had come home yet. Yes, that was probably the best plan.

She hadn't come home by late afternoon or by early evening or by late evening either. The doorman shift changed and still she hadn't returned. Hell, maybe he should have given her *his* number. He was spending his life in front of this building. His hair would turn gray soon, and his teeth begin to fall out.

"You sure she didn't come home yet?" he asked the night doorman for the third time.

For the third time the doorman nodded. This boy cut no ice with him; the man could see that there wasn't going to be a tip in it for him, so why waste words?

"Maybe there's a back way?" asked Tony hopefully.

The doorman didn't even bother to put down his copy of tomorrow's *Daily News*. This kid must really be from hunger if he thought Laura Ravell was going to come in by the back door.

It was getting late, and Tony would soon have to be at work. Desperate times deserve desperate measures, and he cleared his throat with what he thought was some importance.

"Just tell her Mr. Tony Manero dropped by. She knows me, and I'm at The Savage Instinct. Tell her The Savage Instinct, she knows the place. The telephone number there is 555-4897, or 555-4597 . . . or . . . forget it."

This was tantamount to telling a deceased mutt to play dead. The doorman had no intention of not forgetting it, he hadn't even been listening. Dispirited, Tony moved on down the street.

But he wasn't quite ready to go to work yet. He had an hour or so to kill, and he was hungry to share the time with somebody. If not Laura, then maybe Jackie. Sure, why not Jackie? They were friends, weren't they?

Hell, Jackie was working. She was singing at a rock club on the Lower East Side, a neighborhood euphemistically known as the East Village. In the last few years a group of music clubs had sprung up like mushrooms here and there downtown, and like mushrooms they withered early and died. The Mudd Club was one of the few that had achieved any success, but Jackie wasn't singing there. Neither was she at CBGB's. She was at some incredible hole called . . . let him think a minute . . . yeah, Bad News.

Well, why not? He'd been intending to catch her gig, and now was as good a time as any. He hiked over to Lexington and caught the downtown local.

Bad News certainly did live up to its name. It had one claim to fame, if you could call it fame. One rock group spawned there, a collection of punkers called The Spastics, had gone on to something like celebrity, although a fleeting celebrity. The Spastics had cut an album called *Spit in My Eye and Charge Me for the Eyewash,* and the damn thing had taken off. Number thirty with a bullet. The group might have gone on to further fortune if the lead singer, Ookie Pukie, hadn't accidentally put a slug through what passed for his brain, while threatening his latest girlfriend with a Magnum. As it was, the deceased Ookie became something of a minor cult figure to fourteen-year-olds and passed into the trivia of the 1980s, to be collected someday as a fact in a cheap paperback book.

The club had since dragged along dismally, three months behind in its rent, and the only reason it hadn't closed down entirely was that the landlord had found no other tenant to fill the ugly space.

But a gig was a gig, and maybe—just maybe—Mick would drop in some night with Jerry and make the club's rep again. And singing somewhere, anywhere, was probably better than singing nowhere. So Jackie kept on keepin' on, hoping for the best but expecting the worst.

Jackie was singing when Tony entered the Bad News. There was a tiny stage, big enough only to hold her three-piece backup, drums, keyboard, lead guitar. A few scattered patrons, none of them drinking anything more expensive than beer, sat at rickety little tables here and there around the room, barely listening. The club was very dark, which was just as well, because it was hideously decked out with bad murals, and the walls were scabrous with peeling paint and cracked plaster. A few gels made colored lights on the little bandstand, washing out Jackie's delicate beauty and making her look harsh.

She spotted Tony as soon as he came in and gave him a little nod of hello, which he acknowledged with a wave of his hand. He stood at the back of the room listening to her; the song was terrible, but Jackie herself wasn't half-bad. Wasted here though.

When the set was over, Jackie gave a tiny bow to no applause and came down off the platform to talk to Tony.

"Sounds good," he greeted her. "How ya doin'?"

"Fine. Congratulations. I heard you're in the show."

Tony couldn't help a gratified smile. "Yeah, maybe it's starting to happen."

"You on your way to work?" asked Jackie, taking in Tony's bar costume—tuxedo pants and shirt, brocade vest.

"Yeah, I'm gonna give notice," Tony told her happily. Then a thought struck him, something that had been nagging at him for several hours but which had eluded him up to now. "Listen." He looked down at her earnestly. "I got this chorus job on my own, didn't I? I mean, you didn't see anybody say anything to the director or something?"

For the merest fraction of a second, Jackie hesitated. In fact she had been at the theater all afternoon and she *had* seen Jesse and Laura with their heads together, calling Joy over. It was only minutes later that Joy had phoned Tony. But what did that mean? Almost surely it had nothing to do with Tony, right? What was more natural than for the star and the director-choreographer to have their heads together?

"I'm sure you got it on your own," she answered him firmly.

"Wait a minute!" said Tony suddenly, frowning.

"What?"

"Why's he staring at you like that?" Tony was glaring at the guitarist on the bandstand, a young man with freckles.

Jackie shook her head, annoyed. "He's a friend. It doesn't mean anything."

But Tony was incensed, and he shouted angrily at the guitar player, "Hey, you see me talkin' here or what?"

"Tony, don't," Jackie protested, embarrassed. Tony's burst of irritated jealousy had caught her by surprise. It seemed to her so unprovoked she couldn't understand it.

"Don't what?" And again to the other man, he raised his voice. "Don't you see I'm engaged in conversation, or what? Maybe you want me to do a drum solo on your body?" The guitarist raised empty hands to show his lack of interest in a fight.

"What's wrong?" demanded a genuinely puzzled Jackie.

How could Tony explain when he didn't understand it himself? His rage was born partly of his anxieties from the long day and his disappointment at not seeing Laura tonight. He felt cheated of Laura, and he didn't want to be cheated of Jackie too. Even though he no longer wanted her for his lover, he felt possessive of her still. She belonged to him, and nobody else was to lay a hand on her. It was irrational, and he knew it, but he couldn't help it. That's the way he was made. What was once his was always his; in Bay Ridge you were taught never to let go or somebody else would grab it fast.

"Y'know, I got no time for guys that don't show any respect," was what he came up with.

"What? Are you crazy tonight?"

He had to smile at that. "No, I'm emotional," he confessed.

Jackie shook her head, half-amused, half-exasperated. Would Tony never grow up? "Want to meet after work?"

Tony nodded his agreement. He had a fairly early shift tonight, from ten o'clock until one in the morning. Jackie got off at two.

"Yeah, I'll meet you at two out front."

"Out front at two," confirmed the girl.

"Ya gotta commitment," joked Tony. "Ya sound real good." He touched Jackie lightly on the face with genuine affection. Jackie felt the impulse to grab his hand and kiss it, but she suppressed it. A distance had grown up between them almost overnight, and she was pretty sure she knew the reason. Long, long legs and a mass of honey-colored hair. As she watched Tony heading for the door, a stab of heartache took her by surprise. She really didn't want to analyze the depth of her feelings for Tony Manero; what was the use?

Almost to the club door, Tony turned for one last parting shot at the hapless and innocent guitar player. He pointed one finger at him.

"Try American Bandstand!" he yelled.

Despite her heartache, Jackie broke up completely. That Tony! Too much!

*   *   *

There are few opportunities in life one gets to gloat, and Tony wasn't the man to let a single one of them go by unseized. So it was with real delight that he announced to Fred that he was leaving The Savage Instinct, leaving for good. And he wouldn't be back.

Fred was most obviously skeptical. "Yeah? So when are ya gonna quit?"

"I ain't quittin'," Tony retorted rather pompously. "I'm resignating for official reasons."

"What reasons?"

"I'm dancin' in a Broadway show!" Tony exulted.

Fred put one hand over his heart in a dramatic gesture. "Gimme a break!" he scoffed. "You ain't got what it takes!"

Now you can say a lot of things to a lot of people, but you can never tell an Italian boy from Brooklyn that he hasn't got what it takes. Tony's eyes sparked twin blue fires, and his face darkened dangerously.

"Ain't got it?" he demanded incredulously. "Where's ya sister? Find ya sister!"

"Whatta ya doin'?" demanded Fred in his turn, his eyes slits and his cheeks red.

"Where is she?"

"Whatta ya doin'?"

Tony looked angrily around the room until he spotted a pretty dark-haired waitress with sizable breasts.

"Hey, Margaret, c'mere. Come on over."

"Whatta ya *doing?*" Fred's face was puffing up like a blowfish; he looked as though he were about to be carried off by a stroke.

"How ya feeling, Margaret?" asked Tony in a companionable way when the girl approached. "Hey, Margaret, your brother here thinks I ain't got it." He grinned at her.

Margaret grinned back, a smile of great significance. Without taking her eyes off Tony, she said, "He's got plenty, Freddie."

Her brother was gasping for air. "What's that

mean?" he demanded in a strangled voice, glaring at his sister.

"It means what it means, so forget it," she retorted indifferently, picking up a fresh tray of drinks from the bar.

Washing glasses, Tony smiled to himself. The Italians have a saying: revenge is a dish that people of taste prefer to eat cold. Freddie wasn't going to forget Tony Manero in a hurry. Now *who* ain't got it?

He'd washed his last glass, swept his last floor, hung up his bar apron for the last time. Tony and The Savage Instinct had come to the parting of the ways, at least professionally. From now on when he came here, he'd come in through the front door as a patron. Leaving here had been something of a triumph. A small one, granted, but a triumph nonetheless.

But his triumph was tarnished by the fact that he still hadn't seen Laura, and he scooted uptown for one last try.

The night doorman swore for the dozenth time that Miss Ravell was definitely not in, had not come in yet and was probably not coming in for a while. But where the hell was she? It was after two in the morning and freezing cold. Tony felt his behind turning blue, but he was one stubborn man. This time he was determined to wait it out until Laura or the cows came home, whichever was first. He might die of exposure, but he wanted to see his lady.

Pacing in the chilly air, he lost track of the time, so when a voice behind him said, "Tony," he whirled, surprised.

Laura was standing there, looking gorgeous. She was dressed to her fine white teeth. Diamond earrings glistened at the lobes of her ears, and she was wrapped in furs like a Siberian princess. Her hair tumbled around her luscious face in curls Tony longed to reach out and touch with his fingertips.

"How ya doin'?" he managed to croak. God, she was so beautiful!

"Fine," Laura smiled at him casually. "You look like you're freezing to death."

Tony shrugged nervously, "No, I—" He was about to explain that he'd just been passing by a minute ago and thought he'd just happen to see if Laura was home, but he abandoned that lie as too ridiculous.

A car door slammed, and suddenly a man was standing at Laura's side. A tall man, pleasant-faced, with graying hair. He wore a beautiful overcoat of cashmere with a large fur collar, perfect for the icy temperatures. He looked rich. At the curb a long, low limousine, idling, confirmed the impression.

"We all set?" The gray-haired man took Laura's arm in a proprietary way as Tony stared in horror, speechless and embarrassed.

"Mark, this is Tony," Laura said politely, as though Tony were a stranger. "Tony was just hired to be in the show."

"Good," said Mark without interest.

Feeling like he'd just crawled out from under a rock, Tony wanted out of there desperately. He couldn't believe that this was happening to him, that this beautiful woman who had been with him last night was now treating him like the delivery boy from Bendel's. All day long he'd thought of little else but her, and now she was acting like they'd met only this afternoon. He stared at her, willing her to look directly into his face.

But Laura kept her profile to Tony, and refused to let her eyes meet his. "Want to come up for a drink?"

"Are you serious?" he demanded.

"Excuse me?" Laura's words were polite, but the frost that dripped from them was an intense warning.

This was no place for Tony Manero, standing here on the corner like some panhandler, his stomach muscles in a knot, being humiliated by a prima donna who was accidentally the most beautiful and desirable woman in the world.

"I gotta be goin'," he mumbled, his face red.

Laura gave him a noncommittal smile. "All right, then I'll see you at rehearsals. And you'd better get out of the cold before you crack." She swept by him in a cloud of expensive perfume and disappeared into the lobby of her apartment building, the Mark turkey at her side.

"Nice meeting you," Tony said to the empty air. It was one of the worst moments of his life.

Downtown, standing on the corner in front of the Bad News club, Jackie shivered. Tony had said two o'clock, and now it was almost three. Miserably she told herself that he was almost certainly not coming, that he'd been detained somewhere, maybe on business. Maybe he had to work overtime because he was quitting. But then why hadn't he phoned? She was freezing, and this neighborhood was no place for a girl to be out at night alone. Every scummy creep, junkie and wino in a radius of two miles had already tried coming onto her, hitting on her for money. She looked despondently at her watch. Ten to three. Should she give him ten more minutes?

Admit it. He stood you up. That's all there is to it. Wherever he is, whoever he's with, whatever he's doing, he's not thinking of you. He's forgotten you even exist. You've been stood up.

Unwillingly she pictured him cozy and comfortable in some warm, luxurious place with Laura Ravell by his side. They were drinking wine, clinking glasses, and now they were kissing. And now they were . . . Jackie blinked the tears out of her eyes and headed slowly for the subway, for the long, lonely ride home.

It was one of the worst moments of her life.

Chapter Ten

THE FIRST DAY OF REHEARSAL FOR A large Broadway show is like no other experience on earth. For one thing, the noise is unreal. There is intermittent loud music, the heavy thud of the dancers' feet as they block out routines, the yell of the director's voice, which becomes hoarser and shriller as the long day progresses. The stars yell back, probably because they are the only ones in the company who can get away with it. And there is always hammering, sawing and pounding going on somewhere in the theater at union wages, even when the director, choreographer and all the assistants are screaming for quiet. If your nerves cannot stand loud noises, then first rehearsals are not for you.

Everything is chaotic and very ugly. The theater itself, which is gilded and glittering by night, is shabby and worn during the day. You can see the peeling paint, the torn coverings of the seats, the dust, the ancient chewing gum stuck to the floors, the sagging coils that bear the timeworn imprints of thousands of behinds. There are used coffee cups everywhere, and they crunch underfoot because they are made of soft plastic. There are also little plastic stirrers and empty sugar and diet sugar envelopes. Everywhere. On the stage, in the orchestra, in the sound booth, in the wings, behind the flats. A rehearsal, like Napoleon's army, marches on its stomach, but its stomach is filled with coffee.

The dancers themselves are no beauties in rehearsal; they wear heavy layers of clothing to keep their muscles warm, and they sweat constantly. It's hard to find a young man or woman attractive when the hair is pasted to the neck with perspiration and the breath is coming heavily from exertion. There are of course notable exceptions to that rule, such as Laura Ravell, whose beauty was unreal even under the most trying of circumstances, even a first-day rehearsal. Tony kept sneaking glances at her, while Jackie kept sneaking glances at Tony sneaking glances. Laura paid no attention to either of them.

Jesse's rehearsals were different from most other directors', even on the first day, although Tony had no way of knowing this, having no basis for comparison. Most choreographers accept the fact that most dancers think with their feet, but Jesse Benton didn't. Just as the dinosaur had two brains, one to control his tail and the other up in his skull, so Jesse demanded two brains in his dancers. The feet, okay, sure. But a dancer had to have something up there in his skull too. It was part of what Jesse looked for when he hired even the lowliest chorus dancer.

Jesse's concepts for this musical were very definite, and he wanted that to get across right from minute one of day one. Not content with merely blocking out routines on the first day, he wanted his dancers to understand what they were doing and why. This was a complicated show, based loosely on Dante's *Inferno* and *Purgatorio,* and if it didn't exhibit some intelligence along with its heavily sensual content, they might all just as well pack it up and go home right now. Forty dancers had been hired for the show; two principals and nineteen men and nineteen women, only two of each being non-Equity. Tony was one of the two males given the break. As soon as he had his union card, he'd be in a privileged position for his next show.

The two lead dancers were Laura Ravell and a tall blond young man named Butler Willson. Both of them had worked with Jesse before as featured dancers, and neither of them had had to audition, having been signed in advance. The chorus was divided into two lines, with Jackie in the front line and Tony in the back.

If Tony believed his life up to then had been one of toil, he'd never rehearsed with Jesse Benton. Jesse was a slave driver, demanding the utmost from his dancers even on the first day of rehearsal. But he was also a perfectionist, driving himself as hard as he drove the others, so dancers always adored him and would gladly climb over one another's dead bodies to work with him. He understood them, having been one of them for years, and he made them look not only good but great.

They'd been working for several hours now, going over and over the same routine, with Jesse's eagle eyes boring into them, Jesse's voice demanding that they do it again, better this time.

"Get lighter! Get lighter!" he roared at them. "Feel the downbeats! Define the downbeats!"

They tried it again, and it wasn't a whole lot better.

"Enough," Jesse told Joy in great weariness. She stopped the recorded music, and the dancers wound down, rubbing at their necks and shoulders, drying their hair, loosening up tightly bunched muscles. Then they gathered around him like players around a coach.

Jesse looked around the circle of expectant faces and began. "What we have here is a conceptual interpretation problem, which is easy to overcome if you forget you're dancers doing a job for a few bucks! You're translators of body language. That's all dancing is, body language. Therefore the more razor sharp the performance, the more people will understand what we're saying."

Tony was taking the opportunity to study Laura's perfect profile, which was turned toward him. But he was listening to Jesse too, and he turned to Jackie to exchange nods of agreement and try a tentative little smile. Jackie angrily turned her face away.

"So don't waste my time going through the *motions* of emotions," Jesse continued, his dark eyes probing the dancers' faces. *"Feel* what the hell you're doing. For those who forgot, this show is called *Inferno*, a journey through Hell ending with an ascent to Heaven. It may seem simple, but if it's going to work, you've really got to bust your asses! Now, everybody, once again!"

The dancers rose to their feet with renewed energy and moved into formation. As he moved toward his place at the front of the line, Butler Willson found Jesse's hand on his arm, holding him back.

"How do you feel?" Jesse asked his lead dancer.

Butler looked puzzled. "Fine."

"Prove it," Jesse said shortly. "Here we go. One, two, three, four . . ."

This time the routine was sharper, beginning to show a definite shape, like a point emerging under a whittler's knife. Tony was really getting centered, going deep inside himself as he always did when dancing, pulling out his feelings and the emotions he never expressed in words. He was so into the dance that he didn't notice that Jesse's eyes were following him, that Jesse was looking at him in a whole new speculative way.

The day was a long and exhausting one, but ultimately very satisfying. For the first time in his life, Tony could actually believe that he was getting somewhere, that he would be creating something with his life, not just squandering it. Jesse Benton's tireless direction and complex choreography were inspiring him to his best efforts; *this* was what it was all about. *This* was what he'd been working toward, a chance to prove what he was made of.

He dressed quickly without talking to the other dancers; he was determined not to miss Jackie. He owed her a very big, very humble apology. It wasn't until he'd returned to his hotel room that he remembered their date and realized that she must have been standing on an icy street corner for half an hour or more waiting for him. God, sometimes he was so damn stupid! He'd stood up his best friend and on a cold winter night too. No wonder she was angry with him. She had every right to be.

Jackie was coming down the stairs now, her dance bag in her hand. When she saw Tony waiting for her, a look of annoyance crossed her pretty face, a look she couldn't prevent. But she was determined to keep herself under control and not lose her cool. She'd been humiliated enough and saw no need to add more emotional content to this encounter. Besides, from the contrite expression on Tony's handsome face, she had a pretty good idea of why he was standing there waiting.

"About last night," he began, but Jackie interrupted him firmly.

"You don't have to say anything."

Tony gave her his best little-naughty-boy look, guaranteed to melt rock and most of it quite sincere. "If you wanna shoot me—go ahead. I deserve it."

"It's all right," said Jackie carefully, not looking directly at him.

But Tony was shaking his dark head. "It's not," he insisted. "It won't happen no more. I just got hung up. Look. What can I say?"

Jackie felt her lower lip beginning to tremble, and she struggled to control it. "You don't have to say anything," she repeated, refusing to meet Tony's eyes.

"Don't say that. 'Cause when you say that, I know you really want me to say something."

He was right, of course. She *did* want to hash things out once and for all. "What do you want to talk about?"

Tony shrugged. "I don't know. Anything."

Jackie drew in a deep breath, and took the plunge. "Laura."

"Who cares about her?" lied Tony.

Jackie, irritated by Tony's obvious evasions, turned to leave. "I'd better get to Fatima's," she told him shortly.

"You're mad."

"I'm not mad," she said. If he could lie, she could lie.

But Tony wouldn't let her go. "When the veins in your neck start poppin' out, you're definitely very annoyed. C'mon, Jackie. Don't go around thinkin' I'm playing games with you, 'cause I'm not." He just about had himself believing his words, when Laura Ravell came down the steps toward them. Tony broke off, speechless, and Jackie turned to catch him in a moonstruck stare. His look told her everything she had to know, and she felt her heart begin to break inside her body.

"There's the young lovers," said Laura lightly, the thinnest possible edge to her voice. Seeing Tony in such earnest and obviously heavy conversation with Jackie had rekindled Laura's interest in him. She was very like Tony in some ways. She wasn't too interested in what she could have easily, but if somebody else had a prior lien on the property, it became suddenly very desirable. Relationships with Laura were primarily an exercise in personal power. Tony on the other hand was far more simplistic in his approach to women. What he wanted, he took. After he had it, he lost interest, but that didn't mean he was about to yield it up to anyone else. Both Tony and Laura were dogs in the manger, but the significant difference between them was that Tony was unaware of how and why he was acting that way, while Laura was very, very conscious of everything she said and did. Tony really did try to be sincere, and he sometimes succeeded. To Laura, sincerity was unexplored territory and likely to remain so. Where Tony was blunt, Laura was subtle, but to both the upper hand was the only one worth having. Both of them thought of relationships as something like automobiles, and each wanted to be in the driver's seat.

Of the three of them only Jackie knew that relationships are precious and fragile, not to be driven by one person, but to be shared by both. She was willing to give more than she received—with Tony Manero that attitude was mandatory—but she was not willing to give ninety percent when Tony was no longer interested in coming up with the other ten.

Seeing the glance that smoldered now between Laura and Tony, Jackie understood everything, and the bottom fell out of her world.

"I'll see everybody tomorrow," she said very quietly and began to move off.

"Yeah, I'll call ya," Tony responded quickly.

Jackie threw him one last doubting, troubled look and was gone.

Laura stood looking after her with no very pleasant expression on her face. She was gorgeous, her tumbling hair tied up off her brow, her slim body bundled into an expensive fox coat.

"If you're her friend, you should do her a big favor," she told Tony.

"What's that?"

"Help her with her dancing."

Tony rose quickly to Jackie's defense. "There's nothing wrong with her dancin'." His cheeks burned hotly and his eyes were electric blue.

"I really like her," said Laura coolly, "but to be honest, her timing is off, and she's not too inspired. But you, you really looked good."

For the first time in his life, Tony didn't respond to a compliment about his dancing. "Where are you comin' from?" he demanded, scowling.

"Is something wrong?" That beautiful question mark again, with her perfect face and her ice princess manners.

"I don't like being led on," said Tony, giving it to her straight.

"Who's leading you on?"

"I try to call you up, and I can't get your number. I come over, you're not there. I hang around all night, and you come home with some guy. Who're you playin' around with?"

Laura blew her cool completely. "Are you talking to me?" she yelled. "You're not talking to me, are you?!"

"Who do you think I'm talking to?" Tony yelled back.

By now most of the dancers were dressed and on their way home, coming down the stairs and passing Tony and Laura. Tony became conscious suddenly that the two of them were the object of a lot of curious glances, and he looked around for some privacy. Under the stairwell was the most secluded place available, and he stepped into its shadows.

"C'mere," he called urgently to Laura. "I wanna know why you're doing this."

But Laura didn't budge. "I don't have to stand under stairs to talk."

"You don't care if people hear us talkin'?"

Laura gave a deliberate little shrug, and her expression turned twenty degrees warmer. "Why?" she asked him teasingly. "What's the big secret, Tony?"

"It's no secret! It's just that this is nothing to you, right? What we did is nothing, right?" He was desperate to get through to Laura, to establish some ground rules for communication, for continuing this relationship. Laura was like a fever in his blood; she made him weak, and he couldn't shake her.

"It was nice," admitted Laura with a tiny cat smile. Tony shook his head, exasperated. "Nice," he snorted. "Something you do all the time, like having breakfast."

"I usually skip breakfast," laughed Laura. And she turned to go, calling "Later," over her shoulder. She was quite pleased with herself, feeling very much in control of the way things were going. She wanted Tony, but as an occasional diversion, not as a constant companion. And she wanted him on her terms. It was her intention to use him like a television set—turn him on when she wanted a little amusement, switch him off when she had more important things to do. Nothing wrong with that; men manipulated women all the time.

"Where are you going?" Tony demanded. He was no television set, not even for the most beautiful woman he'd ever seen in his life. Nobody switched Tony Manero on and off. He wanted Laura for his lady, to be with and talk to and yes, to wear like a diamond. She was different from anybody he'd known before, and this difference was part of his new life, part of what he'd been working so hard for and striving toward. And here she was, turning her back on him and walking away like he was nobody.

"I said later." The temperature had dropped way down again, and there was ice forming on Laura's words.

Tony leaped forward and grabbed her hard by the arm. "Hey, I'm talkin' to you!"

Quick as a cat, Laura turned and backed away from him, her eyes dark with fury, her face distorted. "Get your bloody hands off me!" she snarled. "Don't you ever put your hand on me! Who the hell do you think you're dealing with? Some backstage groupie who jumps when you call? Is that what you think I am? We met, I liked you. What did you think it was, true love? And you think I used you? What about *you* using *me*? Everybody uses everybody!" She broke off, conscious that she was shrieking like a fishwife, and pulled herself together.

"Later," she said again as she walked away.

Stricken, his fantasies about Laura and himself in shattered ruins at his feet, Tony stood looking after her. Her anger had caught him totally off guard. It seemed to him to be excessive. What had he done that was so terrible? Sure, they'd met and liked each other. Was it so unnatural to go on wanting more? People wanted more from one another all the time. Wanted it and got it. It didn't strike him as ironic that Laura had treated him substantially the same way he'd been treating girls and women all his life. She was simply more openly hostile.

Whenever a woman had wanted more from Tony, he'd run like the wind out the nearest exit. He'd even run from Jackie, for whom he had a genuine feeling and who was obviously nuts about him. Now Tony was hurting because the woman he wanted had turned her back on him, showed him that she and not he was in control, flaunted his feelings openly in front of the rest of the company. It was, as they say in England, a case of the biter bit, but that didn't make it any less painful.

Jackie hadn't gone very far; she was standing just outside the theater door, and she'd heard the entire quarrel. Her thoughts and emotions were in turmoil—anguish over the proof that Laura and Tony were close, pity for Tony's predicament and the ache he must be feeling. Yet she wouldn't have been human if there wasn't the merest trace, just a tiny hint, of satisfaction that Tony was getting back a little of what he'd been dishing out. As the old song goes, "So you met someone and now you know how it feels; goody, goody." But most of all she felt a deep anger and resentment at Laura Ravell. How dare she! She wasn't good enough for Tony. She might be gorgeous, rich and talented, but she was a cold bitch and no mistake. And Tony, for all his conceit, all his macho arrogance, was basically such a sweet, well-meaning kid. Jackie knew there was a lot of love in there somewhere; Tony just didn't know how to let it out. He'd never learned. His entire background—his home, his family, his friends—had all been dedicated to teaching him that men didn't cry, that to act like a man was to constantly have to prove you were stronger and tougher than other men.

There was sensitivity there, Jackie was convinced of it. It showed in Tony's eyes sometimes, in his brooding face, in his desperate need to succeed. It was love he was after, universal love and approval. And truly selfish, insensitive people, take Ms. Rich Ravell as an excellent example, don't give two cents for anybody's love and approval, because they don't need it.

Jackie ached to go to Tony and take him in her arms, but she knew that this was the last thing he could possibly tolerate, pity from the girl he'd lied to. Pity in any form made him crazy; now it would be more than he could bear.

So she'd have to ache in private, pretend she'd heard nothing, seen nothing, knew nothing. Besides, it was over, wasn't it, between Laura and Tony? Tony could never go back to her now, now that she'd trashed him in public and told him to keep his hands to himself. So, thought Jackie sadly, all she'd have to do was wait. Maybe Tony would come back to her after all. If she was good, if she was patient. She sighed.

But Jackie wasn't the only one who had seen and heard everything. In the shadows at the top of the stairs, Jesse Benton, himself unseen, had watched the anger rising between his star and a chorus boy, and it had put the glimmering of an idea into his head. Just the glimmering.

Chapter Eleven

REHEARSALS PROGRESSED, BUT JESSE WAS not satisfied. Something was wrong, something central to the show, and it was bugging him more and more with every day that passed. It wasn't that people weren't working hard; they were. They always worked their hardest for Jesse, and he took that for granted. But there was something missing . . . and he was almost afraid to identify what it was, as one avoids touching the exposed nerve in a tooth with one's tongue.

He had hired Butler Willson the same way he'd hired Laura Ravell, without an audition. Why not? It was done all the time with principal dancers. Both of them had worked for him before, both very, very good. Laura was exceptionally good, but Butler was a fine dancer with a made reputation. Maybe the problem was that Laura was exceptional and Butler wasn't. Excellent, but not exceptional. Laura moved across the stage like a burning flame, and Butler was sometimes the wet blanket that put the fire out.

In the show Laura and Butler had several astonishing *pas de deux,* intricately choreographed duets between two magnificent bodies. These were the great set pieces of *Inferno.* If they did not come off as incredibly sexual, charged with high-voltage electricity, then the show would lose its center and be flabby and boring.

A fortune was being spent on the technical effects for this show. Nothing like it had ever been seen on stage before; it was absolutely state of the art. Laser technology, complicated lighting and sound effects. At the outset one of the money men had joked that the stage manager ought to have an engineering degree to protect their investments, and Jesse, his eyes narrowed, had taken the advice quite seriously and had gone out and found himself a union stage manager who also held an M.A. from MIT. But all the high-tech razzle-dazzle would be dollars flushed down the toilet if the dances were not perfectly executed and totally believable in their sexuality.

What Butler lacked was sexuality. Tall, handsome, blond and clean-cut, he was like white bread, especially when matched with the fiery glory of Laura's looks. She sizzled; he just fizzled. Between them there was no body heat, no chemistry. The two of them didn't look as though they couldn't keep their hands off each other.

Antagonism in its classical sense was what Jesse was trying to achieve on stage. This was to be the struggle between good and evil, the struggle for that most precious thing of all, the human immortal soul. If that struggle was not real, if the attraction and repulsion didn't come across to the audience like a blast from a live furnace, then the show could not possibly succeed in Jesse's terms. It might even be a hit, a box-office smash, but to Jesse Benton the perfectionist it would be a total failure, a thing without heart or life.

Over and over again Jesse put Laura and Butler

through their first *pas de deux*. The steps were right, but still he caviled, looking for a perfection that he was now unsure the dancers could give him.

"Stop!" he called suddenly. "Enough, enough!" He strode across the stage to where his lead dancers were standing. "I'm not sure if this is getting across what I want. Look, Butler, watch me carefully."

Tony also was watching carefully; he never took his eyes off Laura while she was dancing. Even if his body didn't still crave hers, he'd be looking at her. Her dancing was pure beauty, a thing apart from her, yet very much a part of her, a thing of air and fire, of spirit and flesh. Butler he thought only fair. Fair. What Tony couldn't understand was how any man—straight, gay or whatever—could dance with a woman like Laura without a total involvement. What went on between them ought to be a positive, not a negative. But he saw nothing between Butler and Laura but skill and practice.

Now Jesse, demonstrating to Butler what he was driving at, grabbed Laura around the waist suddenly, his fingers digging slightly into the flesh.

Laura gave a little jump and a giggle.

"Still ticklish, huh?" He smiled at her.

Still ticklish? The words burned themselves into Tony's brain, and his eyes widened involuntarily. He took a good long look at Jesse and Laura and it flashed on him with sudden certainty that they had once been lovers. There was a telltale familiarity in his touch and in her reaction to it. And there was chemistry between them still, a flirtatiousness that made Tony do a slow burn, watching, eating his heart out.

Now Jesse was showing Butler the way he wanted him to do the routine, and even in the demonstration there was a sexuality about the dance that Tony recognized at once and that Butler had not been achieving.

"What I want here is a much more forceful movement, like this," he said, grabbing Laura and spinning her to one side. He bent her back at the waist and grabbed her by the hair, then whipped her into an upright position. It was only the work of two seconds, but it possessed an authority of movement that established Jesse, not Laura, as the dominant partner and restored the entire balance of the routine.

"This is a very sensual show," Jesse said to Butler, "so what the hell! Be sensual! There's no law against it. Now you try it."

"No problem," Butler said coolly, and worked through the move with almost military precision. It was technically perfect, but it lacked fire.

Jesse shook his head. "Stronger!" he ordered. "You're not going to break her."

"I'll get it." Mr. White Bread showed his teeth in a big wholesome smile. "No problem."

No problem, but no passion, either.

Jesse sighed. Had he made a mistake hiring Butler? He had thought the contrast between them would be perfect, Butler as the pale soul and Laura as the vivid temptress, demon, dominatrix. But somehow the combination wasn't working.

Turning to Joy, Jesse ordered, "From the top."

"First positions," called Joy, and the dancers took their opening stances.

"What are ya doin' after work?" Tony whispered to Jackie.

"I've got some 'commitments,'" said Jackie crisply.

Tony flashed his smile. "No, ya don't."

But Jackie answered quietly, "Yes, I do," and his smile vanished.

"Think about what you're doing!" called Jesse, and Tony gave the work his full attention. Funny, when he was teaching and bartending and running to auditions, he wasn't working half as hard as he was working now, and he was always twice as tired. But no matter how hard Jesse pushed them, Tony came up thirsting for more. He was stretching, reaching, both inside and outside himself, working like a dog to attain that single measure of perfection, and it exhilarated him and energized him. Now if he could only get his personal life in order.

Tony's personal life had never presented a problem except when there was more of it than one man—even a superman like Tony—could handle. All the women were pretty much alike. Until Jackie. She had been special, and she was special still. Except that she had made the mistake of falling in love with him and wanting a closeness and an intimacy that Tony couldn't handle. So how much closer could they get? That had been his attitude then, and ironically enough he was paying for it now. Because he was seeing for the first time how much closer it was possible to get. He wanted closeness now, and oddly he wanted it with both Laura and Jackie. He hated the distance between him and Jackie that had grown up since the affair with Laura. He missed Jackie, missed the camaraderie and the understanding that he'd undervalued. There was that middle western wisdom again—the well was dry and Tony was missing the water.

As for Laura, once burned twice shy was the rule, but Tony was the exception that proves the rule. He couldn't keep his eyes off her, even now while he was dancing.

"Five, six, seven, eight!" barked Jesse, counting the downbeats, emphasizing them with a slap of his hand on his table. And Tony did the steps, with the corners of his eyes watching out for that glorious body and that tumbling silky hair.

Jackie. Laura. He wanted them both, and he didn't have either one of them. What a new situation for the Italian prince of Bay Ridge! How the fellas from the neighborhood would howl with laughter to know that Tony Manero was having woman trouble!

"How about I come by about nine?" This was the closest he'd ever come to begging, and Jackie bit at her lower lip. If only she could trust him!

"I don't know," she told him finally.

"C'mon, Jackie." All his powers of persuasion were in those two words. Rehearsal was over and he needed to be with somebody. Jackie gave him a suspicious look out of her sea green eyes. "Sure you'll be there?"

Tony grinned broadly. "Yeah, definitely. We'll go out."

"Christmas caroling," joked Jackie.

"How'd you know?" Tony joked back.

Defeated, Jackie nodded her assent. "All right. I'll see you later."

"Remember," called Tony after her. "Don't talk to strangers."

Jackie turned and gave him attitude. "Tony, there is *nobody* stranger than you!"

The famous limousine was waiting at the curb outside the rehearsal studio, and suddenly Laura appeared on her way toward it. She was still in rehearsal clothes—tights and leg warmers over high-heeled sandals—but she'd thrown her fox fur over the costume and looked like a million before taxes.

"Tony."

"Yeah." He regarded her as suspiciously as Jackie had eyed him only minutes before.

Jackie turned at the corner to wave once more to Tony, and saw him talking to Laura. The glow faded from her cheeks, and her hand dropped helplessly to her side. *Not again. Oh, please. Not again.*

Her voice was surprisingly friendly, even warm. "I'm having a few people over tonight. Sort of a pre-Christmas party type thing. Would you like to come?"

Tony stood eyeing her, hanging on desperately to his celebrated cool. "Didn't we have a big fight?" he wanted to know. "Wasn't that you?"

Laura smiled and shook her head. "Not quite. *We* didn't have a fight, *you* did. But now that's hopefully resolved, I'd like to see you again."

He wanted to say no. With every nerve ending in his

body, he willed himself to say no. "What time?" he asked.

"Ten."

Tony forced a shrug. "I don't know," was the best he could manage, the closest to no.

Laura nodded and stepped neatly into the limo.

Wishing he could cut his tongue out, Tony asked again, "Whose limo?"

"See you at ten," she said sweetly. And the car pulled away from the curb with a powerful surge of its noiseless engine.

And one more time Tony forgot all about Jackie, thanks to Laura.

Dressing up for Tony was like a matador donning his suit of lights; it was a ceremonial, almost religious occasion. He hadn't dressed up to go out in a very long time, but a party at Laura's Park Avenue pad was definitely going out. Since his four years of hard work, Tony had added almost nothing new to his wardrobe other than what he needed to get him through the day. But he was still steeped in the Manero style, and this was a special occasion that called for it.

From his former days in Brooklyn as king of the discos, he had almost nothing left. The shirts had all been worn to shreds long ago; the shoes were cracked and broken and had been fed to the garbage dump. But the suit he had kept. The famous Saturday night suit, sparkling white, three-piece with peaked lapels, fitting close to his body, making him outstanding in any crowd. Black hair, white suit, blue eyes. It was cleaned and pressed always. If Tony had to go without food for a week, that suit would be dry-cleaned and pressed.

Reverently he unzipped the aging garment bag and lifted out the suit. It was spotless, just as it ought to be, with trouser creases sharp enough to cut bread. Man, a suit like this would never go out of style!

But would it fit? Tony felt a sudden thrill of horror.

He'd lost weight; in Bay Ridge he'd been ten pounds heavier. His heart in his mouth, he slipped the jacket on.

Perfect. What he'd lost in blubber he'd put on in muscle, and the suit jacket hugged his shoulders and tapered at his waist. The pants might be a little loose in the waist, but his thighs were more powerful than ever and looked incredibly muscular under the white fabric. The vest covered the loose waist.

But what about a shirt? Did he have a shirt good enough for Park Avenue? The dark blue one, it brought out the color of his eyes. Hell! It was at the cleaner's, and they were already closed. The black one . . . no, the pale pink one . . . no, the black one. In a fever of indecision, he tried on and discarded every shirt he owned. Collar up. Collar down. Sleeve cuffs showing. No cuffs. It took him an hour before he was satisfied that he could pass inspection, and he was wearing the black shirt after all. The first one he'd chosen.

Carefully he closed the door of his room on the tangled mess of shirts. Tomorrow. He'd worry about them tomorrow. Tonight was for fun.

The doorman at Laura's building pretended not to recognize him from the other night and challenged Tony like a buck private on guard duty.

"Where to?"

What's the password? thought Tony. "Laura Ravell's place."

"Are you expected?"

"To do what?" A tiny triumph perhaps, but one of the few he'd had lately.

Laura's apartment was tightly packed with people. The last time he'd seen it . . . the only other time . . . it had been vast and cavernous. Now the throng of guests made it look much smaller. A stranger opened the door to him, a weird-looking woman in a turban topped by an egret feather. Laura was nowhere to be seen.

"I'm looking for Laura," Tony said, stepping into the apartment.

The woman shrugged indifferently. "She's here somewhere."

O. J. Simpson couldn't get across that room without a strong backup. Wall-to-wall people, all talking at once, all drinking at once. Cigarette smoke made the air unbreathable, and Tony made instinctively for the balcony. Air. He had to breathe.

But he hadn't gained more than a few feet, not even a first down, when he saw Laura coming in from the balcony. She was breathtaking in something lustrous and silky that appeared to have no seams, no beginning, no ending, and fit her slim body like a second skin. Laura. Finally.

Tony opened his mouth to call to her, then shut it again when Jesse Benton came in directly after her, his hand protectively on her waist. She half turned her head to say something to him, and the smile on her face was so intimate that it was a pail of ice-cold water thrown over Tony's head.

He gasped from the shock of seeing them together, and his hands instinctively balled themselves into fists. For an instant he thought of making a scene, of yelling, of telling Jesse where to get off, of quitting the show. But only for an instant, because he knew it was impossible. The old Tony could do it, maybe, flush everything down the john with some rash words from his big mouth. But the new Tony was more mature and realized the impossibility of a scene. Nobody would gain, and everybody would lose, especially him.

He wanted to go and took a step toward the door. But one step was all he was allowed to take; the doorway was jammed with so many people he couldn't take another.

No. He changed his mind. He didn't want to go; why should he go? He was invited, wasn't he? A guest, as good as any other guest? Any other except Jesse, who was obviously Laura's date. A small voice of reason reminded Tony that he'd been invited, but nothing had been said about his being Laura's date. He'd simply assumed.

Well, didn't he have a right to assume? Was he some kind of yoyo, to be pulled up and down on a string and made to do tricks? Angrily he pushed his way over to the bar using his elbows where necessary and ordered a drink from the redheaded bartender hired for the party.

"I was wondering where you were." Laura had come up behind him. "You look nice."

Fuming, he turned to her, but he kept his voice discreetly low. "I don't believe this."

"What?"

"This!" Tony waved an angry hand in the direction of Jesse, who was talking to an art critic across the room. "You . . . you bring me up here and you're with the director."

Laura rolled her eyes heavenward in exasperation.

"Didn't you learn anything from the other day?" She put one hand on Tony's arm, but he jerked it away in fury. "Didn't you?"

Across the room Jesse kept the conversation going, but only with half an ear. He kept a careful eye on Laura and Tony, aware that yet another confrontation was taking place between them.

They moved away from the bar. Laura gnawed her lip but was much calmer than Tony.

"If you want to leave, leave. It's your choice," she told him. "Look, maybe you'd better go."

"What's the matter with you?" demanded Tony.

"Excuse me?" Laura looked startled.

"You think you can play with people whenever you want."

Laura looked nervously over her shoulder to make certain that none of her chichi theater or art world friends were hearing any of this, and taking Tony's elbow, guided him down a long corridor to the back of the apartment. There were caterers working in the kitchen and waiters going in and out, and the back door was open to the service part of the building. Laura pulled Tony out into the hallway.

"Look, I'm not playing with anyone. I invited you to a party because in a way I thought you were interesting. Most of these people are interesting. What are you upset about? There's a lot of nice-looking girls here."

"I came here to be with you," said Tony through gritted teeth.

Laura ignored his anger. "I'm with someone else." It all seemed very simple to her. She took the best and left the rest, that was her way of life. A few nights ago she was with Tony, and tonight she was with Jesse. Why was that so hard for Tony to understand and accept?

"How can you keep doin' this?" Tony's frustration was welling up into his throat, choking him with its bile.

Pressing her beautiful lips together, Laura looked him straight in the eye. "If you mean living the way I choose to? Hopefully for a long time. Do you think you have a right to change that? Do you?"

Tony turned his face away, scowling. "Why did we ever bother startin' up if we were always gonna have these problems?"

She shrugged her shoulders. "You came to me, I didn't come to you—"

Tony swung back to face her, interrupting angrily.

"You didn't do nothin', huh? It was all me, right?"

Now Laura was getting bored. This conversation had gone on long enough. "Whatever," she said with indifference. "All I know is I'm getting cold. Look, if nothing else comes of this, you've ended up with a couple of interesting chapters for your diary." She turned to walk away. "You know the way out, don't you?"

It was always the same; it never, never changed. He

lost his temper; she walked out. What kept him going back for more? And why did she keep letting him?

This was nowhere. It was time to go. For the first time this evening, he remembered Jackie, remembering, too, that he'd stood her up again. Jeez, no! *I should get my head examined.*

It came to him suddenly and very clearly that what Laura had been doing to him, he'd been doing to Jackie. Only with less style. That's what hurt the most; Laura had more class than he did. He was tired of being a yoyo for Laura, and all the while he'd been jerking little Jackie up and down, up and down, on a string of his own choosing. Please see me. Oops, sorry, forgot. Forgive me. Where was the difference? The difference was that Jackie was a much better person than he was. Her words were echoing in his ears right now. "Don't play games, Tony. Please don't play games with me."

Don't play games, Laura. Please don't play games with me.

Wow. He deserved all he got, didn't he? Feeling so sorry for himself because Laura was . . . pulling a Tony.

Only Jackie didn't deserve to be treated like that. She'd been loyal, a loyal friend. It had never occurred to Tony before that, just as he couldn't trust Laura, so Jackie couldn't trust him. He'd let her down again and again.

So far all he'd gotten from Laura was a lotta pain.

So far all Jackie had gotten from Tony was a lotta pain.

Jeez, that hurt! He couldn't face that knowledge. But he had to. He had to stop running away from himself and face a few truths. He was so ashamed. He'd acted like a prize idiot, not once, but over and over again. And he'd thought he was being so cool, not wanting to hurt Jackie. He hurt her every time he opened up his big mouth and out popped another half-truth, another self-deception.

He wanted to crawl into a hole and pull it over him. It wasn't only that he'd ignored Jackie's feelings, he'd ignored his own. He'd betrayed her, but also himself. Why had he never seen that before?

He had to find Jackie right now, this very minute, and make it up to her, beg her to forgive him. It wasn't only a matter of another standup; it was all the emotional standups of the past few years he wanted to apologize for. It was all the times he'd burned her, asking for her trust and letting her down and thinking he was doing her a favor!

How could he have been so blind, so damn stupid? *Wow, she's gonna kill me. But I deserve it. There's nothing she can't call me; it's all true.*

He looked at his watch. Jackie would be working now, still on that scroungy little bandstand in the seedy Bad News club.

He headed down Park Avenue and walked east to the subway. There was snow in the air; he could feel it and smell it. The sky was heavy with night clouds, and the temperature was dropping fast. Christmas would be here any minute.

And he and Jackie were gonna go caroling.

The feeble handful of Christmas decorations in the club was in sharp contrast to the huge tree trimmed in silver and white that had dominated Laura's living room tonight. This place was pathetic. Only a bulldozer could make it look better.

Jackie was singing when Tony walked in, his collar up over his freezing ears. He waited until the song was over and came up to her instantly.

"Hey, Jackie, I'm sorry."

"I don't want to see you tonight, Tony." Jackie's voice was so flat and emotionless that it scared him. Anger he could deal with, indignation he could take, but the blankness in her face when she looked at him was terrifying.

"I forgot to call. I'm sorry."

"Tony, I know you are, but you can't treat me like this anymore."

"I won't," promised Tony, and for the first time, it was true.

"I can't always be your second choice."

"You're not!"

Now the blank facade crumpled and Jackie's face was wet with her tears. "Yes, I am, and you know I am," she sobbed.

"I swear it won't happen again!" He reached for her hand, but she pulled it away from him.

"It *will*," she wailed. "It will if I let you. Do you know how many times you've done this? I love you, don't you know that? And . . . and . . . you keep treating me this way." She fought to gain control of herself, but it was impossible.

It was killing him to see her cry like this, killing him to hear her tell him she loved him. He loved her too, but still he wasn't certain how much or in what way. Only that she was Jackie, and that she had been deeply wounded by his own hand. He'd never felt so helpless or alone in his life. Or so scared. All the emotions he'd fought so long to suppress rushed in on him like a tidal wave, shaking him to his very foundations.

"I . . . I don't know what to say." And his voice trembled, very close to tears. Tony Manero in tears!

Jackie was dabbing at her eyes with the sleeve of her blouse. "Don't say anything. I'll be your friend, but no more than that. I have to go now. I have to sing another set."

Tony sighed deeply, accepting her decision, not realizing yet how deeply it cut him. Nodding, he backed away out the door, watching Jackie slowly climb up on that tiny platform to give an indifferent audience yet another piece of her soul. He was unutterably sad.

He tried again later that night, after he knew that Jackie must be home from the club. Using his key, he let himself in downstairs, but he knew he didn't have the right to use the key to Jackie's apartment. Instead he climbed the stairs and knocked on the door.

"Hey, Jackie, I'm sorry," he called.

"I don't want to see you tonight, Tony."

What could he do? He had to accept her decision. To push her any further would be an insult to her intelligence and to her feelings. Ah, maybe tomorrow she'd feel different, he thought with little hope.

The night was very cold; a few flakes of snow were beginning to swirl in the air, the harbinger of more to come.

Tony was alone. And very lonely. Where could he go? What doors would be open to him? None that he really wanted.

Except . . .

He could always go home.

Chapter Twelve

CROSSING THAT BRIDGE ON CHRISTMAS Eve was maybe the hardest thing Tony had ever done. It was going back to Bay Ridge with his tail between his legs, just as he'd always sworn he'd never do. What he'd dreamed of was himself coming back home in a Cadillac a block long, wearing silk suits and a Cartier watch, with a face and style the whole world recognized. A star. Instead here he was, a failure.

Oh, sure, he was working in a Broadway show at last, but what about everything else? In every other facet of his life, Tony had to admit defeat. Funny, he'd been wrong about pretty near everything he'd ever believed in. His values had been shot out of the water and turned out to be not so much values as price tags. He had always tried for the brass ring, and nobody had ever pointed out to him that even if he caught it, brass would turn his finger green. Gold was the only thing that endured, and you didn't find gold riding round and round on a carousel of making out. Gold was rare; you not only had to dig for it, you had to be able to recognize it when you struck it. *Make new friends, but keep the old; the one is silver, the other, gold.* Somebody had written that in Tony's autograph book when he'd graduated from elementary school, Saint Rose of Lima. Why did he remember that now? It was true, though.

God only knows why Tony decided to walk to Brooklyn. He was so despondent, so morose when he left Jackie's house that he couldn't stand to think of the subway. The most depressing place in the world is the BMT on Christmas Eve. All those sad people wishing they were home already, and the graffiti turning the trains into nightmares that moved. He just naturally started to walk downtown, his hands shoved as deeply as possible into the pockets of his leather jacket, shivering in the flurries of snow.

By the time he'd reached the Brooklyn Bridge the snow had stopped falling, leaving a thin crust of diamonds brushed lightly over everything. New York was silent and beautiful; it was either very late or very early, depending on whether you were going to bed or getting up. It was six in the morning, Christmas Day.

Tony loved the Brooklyn Bridge; it was exactly a hundred years old and beginning to look it. But he loved the singing of the wind through the heavy cables like an angel's giant harp. It was cold over the river, though. The wind had risen and Tony discovered that he was colder than he'd ever been in his life. He jogged a little to keep the blood flowing, and when he got off the bridge on the Brooklyn side, he dived into the nearest subway entrance and was lucky enough to catch a local to Bay Ridge within three minutes. A miracle. A Christmas Day miracle.

The house was very quiet at 6:45 in the morning. Anyway who was there to make noise? Only his mother, and she was still upstairs in bed, her hair in rollers.

Using his key, he let himself into the house as quietly as he could and tiptoed up the stairs without turning on a light. In his own room he didn't even bother to hang up his precious white suit; he threw it across a chair and threw his body across the bed and was out like a light.

Tony slept for five hours, waking to a Christmas more depressing than any he could remember. With his mother alone in the house, no husband, no kids, who was there to buy a tree for? So no tree. The house itself with a few bits of Christmas garland and a little white Styrofoam tree on the coffee table was much smaller than he remembered it, even though now that it was empty, it ought to be looking bigger.

Mrs. Manero was of course delighted to see him and made a big fuss over him, stuffing him with all the food she could rustle up at short notice. She too looked smaller than Tony remembered, although he'd seen her a couple of months before. Solitary confinement was making an old woman out of his mother, shrinking her bones and caving in her cheeks, painting big black circles under her eyes.

What was there to do in Brooklyn on Christmas Day? Mrs. Manero attended Mass of course, in her best coat and hat, her rosary wrapped around her fist. It was very clear that she longed to have Tony go with her; it had been such a long time since he'd been to church. He wished he could accommodate her, he really did. But something held him back. Caught in the grip of a listlessness that went bone deep, he didn't want to bring that frame of mind into a church.

So while his mother was at Mass, Tony sat in the little dinette watching dumb children's specials on television, garish and mindless entertainments that appeared to be populated solely by animated blue elves.

When she returned from church, Mrs. Manero went directly into the kitchen, where she stayed for three hours, with the smell of sauce and ham and cinnamon wafting out. She was cooking more food than two people could finish in a week. Cooking calmed her nerves. It was at least something she could deal with.

As for dealing with Tony, she was entirely at a loss.

She'd never seen him this way, hollow-cheeked and sad-eyed, silent and abstracted. What was New York City doing to her boy? He hadn't smiled once in hours, and he didn't even have one argumentative word. That wasn't her Tony, sitting at the table dutifully eating too much without his usual complaints.

She had nothing to say to him, nor he to her, it seemed. They were strangers. Look at him, sitting in front of the TV just like a little old man, watching junk. Something was eating on him, and she had no idea what it was. Only that he was unhappy, very unhappy.

"You want anything, Tony?"

"No, I'm full."

"You want apple pie?" Food was a safe topic, common ground.

"I'm full," he said again, but without irritation. That was so unlike him that Mrs. Manero's heart filled up with worry.

She produced the apple pie. "Eat it," she pleaded. "I made it special."

"I'm not too hungry," said Tony quietly.

Rejected, his mother tried not to show her hurt.

"Hell with it. I'll put it away. I'll have it for lunch, who knows."

Tony looked around the room. "Ya know something?"

"What?"

"The house here looks a lot smaller than when I lived here."

"Smaller?" What was he driving at? Of course it looked smaller. *He* was smaller then, and everything around him was bigger.

"Smaller. You know, the opposite of bigger." The ghost of his familiar arrogance passed briefly across his face.

"So what do you want me to do, Tony? Stretch it?"

Tony shrugged. "I was just making an observation."

For a long minute a strained silence fell between them. Then Tony broke it with an awkward apology.

"Listen, I didn't get a chance to get ya a present. Every store I went to was closed. I'll get ya somethin' good next year."

Mrs. Manero shook her head, amused. "Don't worry about it." Since when did he ever buy her anything? All his money always went onto his own back.

"Are you all right here?" Tony asked suddenly. "Living alone?"

What did he want her to say? The truth? No, Tony, it's a living hell. I'm half out of my mind with loneliness. Instead she said in a low voice, "I got a nice job. It's quiet. Believe me, it's better than ever." Then looking at him sharply, she asked abruptly, "Tony, why'd you come here?"

" 'Cause it's Christmas." He tried to smile, but didn't quite make it.

"Ya weren't here last Christmas. What is it?"

It was a direct question, and Tony didn't want to evade it. He turned to his mother, seeing the wrinkles around her eyes and the deep lines on either side of her mouth. Many new strands of gray had invaded her hair that used to be as black as his own. "I wanted to talk to you, because I've been thinkin' a lotta things."

"Like what things?" She was half-curious, half-skeptical.

Tony searched for the right words. "Things," he said, putting his hands out palms up. "Y'know, the way I always treated everybody. Always putting down everything . . . being hard with you . . . I was just doin' this act thing. So I wanna let you know that."

Mrs. Manero glanced at him sharply, trying to read her son's face. "Are you kiddin'?"

Tony looked her directly in the eye. "No," he told her quietly. "I'm apologizin'."

Mrs. Manero's brows shot up. "Apologizin' for what? Are you sayin' that wasn't the real you back then?"

Tony nodded. "Yeah. It was just an attitude," he admitted.

A loud scoffing laugh broke from his mother's lips, a real laugh, rich with mirth. "I don't believe this!"

Laughter was the last thing that Tony expected. Here he was in a contrite, confessing mood, and his own mother was laughing at him.

"Why not? Believe it."

His mother gave him a long, level look. "I don't, so don't get fresh with me. Your 'attitude' is what got ya outta this neighborhood. So whaddya feeling guilty about? Ya must've been doing something right."

This was a new theory to Tony, and he looked at it carefully, turning it over in his mind, testing it out.

"So what you're sayin'," he said slowly, "is that I've always been a creep, but it's okay because it comes natural."

Mrs. Manero thought about it for a few seconds.

"Something like that," she agreed.

A large, brilliant smile appeared on Tony's face. "Yeah?"

Mrs. Manero smiled back at her son. "Yeah. Double yeah."

It was as though a great weight had been lifted off him. He felt lighter, younger and suddenly hungry again.

"Ma, can I have a piece of that pie?"

Tony returned to work the day after Christmas in a new frame of mind. He seemed older and more serious and a good deal less of a clown. Impressing others no longer appeared to be his top priority, and he kept himself to himself. He didn't seek Jackie out, but neither did he avoid her. He was friendly, polite, warm even, but the spigot that had been labeled "charm" appeared to have been turned off. And his little attention-demanding "watch-me" tricks were no longer in evidence. It really looked as though he were trying to cut down hard on the bull. Tony Manero without bull. Hard to believe.

Laura he didn't look at once. It was as though she had ceased to exist for him, had become just one more dancer in the show.

The work was everything to him now. He concentrated on his steps ferociously, refining his body movements until every angle of his body felt right in every step. This he did for himself alone; he was not even conscious that Jesse's eye was more and more upon him.

They were rehearsing longer and longer hours as opening night loomed nearer. By now every dancer was letter-perfect, the routines so imprinted on their bodies that they could perform them in their sleep.

The only fly in the ointment was still Butler Willson. He still danced with Laura as though he were dancing with himself in a mirror, a shadow dancer. The magnificent woman in his arms didn't seem real to him, but rather a piece of lovely furniture he moved around. Interaction between Butler and Laura was nil.

Realizing that Jesse was not too happy with the state of things, Butler became more and more nervous. Once he forgot the sequence of an important part of the routine and whirled off in the wrong direction, leaving Laura stranded.

"Hold it!" hollered Jesse, his eyes black daggers. Everything stopped on the instant.

"I . . . uh . . . I thought we decided to go downstage," stammered the redfaced Butler.

"That's true," said Jesse, with a dangerous edge to his voice, "but then we decided to go *upstage*."

Butler was so rattled that he became defensive and committed cardinal sin number one. "It was better going downstage," he told the director.

Dancers don't direct. Directors direct. Dancers dance where they're told, when they're told and how they're told by directors.

"Was it?" asked Jesse softly. The bait was laid.

"Much better." The bait was taken.

"I'll tell you what is even better than that," snarled Jesse, springing the trap on the hapless dancer. "Learning the routine the way it's been laid out!"

Butler scampered upstage like a frightened mouse.

"Again!" roared Jesse. "First position! And five, six, seven, eight, do it!"

They did it.

"How do your legs feel?" Tony asked Jackie after the rehearsal had finally come to an end.

"Good. And yours?"

"Not bad."

"That's good." They were practicing being "friends, but nothing more," the way Jackie had decreed, and it had its awkward, superpolite moments.

Laura was deep in conversation with Jesse, but she looked up long enough to throw Jackie a look filled with venom.

"I don't know what you did, but she looks like she hates me," remarked Jackie to Tony.

"I didn't do anything."

The skeptical eyebrow went up. "I'll see you tomorrow," Jackie said briskly. "And stop lying. It's getting to be a bad habit."

"Bad, huh?"

"Very," nodded the girl. "And the worst part is that you're not even good at it."

"I'll practice more," Tony promised. "So you're meeting somebody, right?"

"Yes."

Now it was Tony's turn to be surprised, and his black brows shot up to his sweatband. "You are? I was just kidding."

"I'm not," said Jackie with total cool.

"Like, this somebody you're meetin' wouldn't happen to be a male somebody?"

"Why not?"

"Look, I'm not sayin' anything's wrong with that,

but ya gotta be careful who ya socialize with, because what you think perhaps is a normal-lookin' guy could be nothin' but a professional degenerate." A bit of the old Tony was reaching out to her again.

"I'll be careful," said Jackie. "See you."

Wow. She was moving so fast Tony nearly got knocked down by the breeze. "Wait, listen. I just wanna ask you a favor."

Where the hell did he get his nerve? "What favor?" asked Jackie, incredulous.

"Can you meet me here tonight, about ten?"

Oh, no. Not again. Here we go. Standup City, next stop.

"I don't think I can."

"C'mon," Tony pleaded. "It'll only take a couple of hours."

Jackie gave him the fish-eye. "What if you don't show?" *Which you won't.*

"I'll show. Jackie, I'll owe ya for life. Look, I know I treated ya bad. I've got bad manners. Everybody I hung out with had bad manners, so it's natural that sometimes I do bad things. But I'm tellin ya—" and his large blue eyes looked solemn "—that inside here" . . . and he tapped at his chest . . . "is this gentleman waitin' to get out. How about it?"

I must be crazy, thought Jackie, *but he sounds sincere. He actually sounds sincere.* Shaking her head no, she smiled the little smile that meant yes.

"Thanks," said Tony simply. "Thanks."

Not only did Tony show, but he arrived before ten and was waiting fifteen full minutes for Jackie to show. Now it was his turn to be nervous. What if she didn't come?

He was wearing his rehearsal clothes, and he did a few stretching exercises at the barre, his eyes on himself in the mirror. She was late. Maybe she wouldn't come at all. Maybe she was giving him a taste of his own medicine. Well, he supposed it would serve him right, but he really did want her to be here. He needed her.

Just as he was about to give up and go home, he heard the sounds of footsteps approaching the rehearsal hall. The door opened, and Jackie came in, carrying her dance bag. And she wasn't alone. With her was a tall, good-looking all-American boy in his late twenties.

So she hadn't been fooling. She really *was* seeing somebody. Now why did that make him feel so awkward?

"I didn't think you were coming."

"The show ran late. Tony, this is Carl. Carl, this is Tony. Tony, can I ask you something?"

Tony shook his head. "I gotta ask *you* somethin'."

He waved Jackie closer and lowered his voice to a whisper. "He's got wavy hair."

"So?" Jackie looked at him blankly.

"So, I didn't think you were the wavy hair type," said Tony solemnly, shaking his head of straight black hair. "I never thought that."

Jackie gave a little shrug. "He plays rhythm guitar at the club. He walked me over."

"Rhythm guitar, huh?"

"Rhythm guitar. Why?"

"Why?" Tony's eyes widened in mock disbelief. "What's the matter with you, Jackie? Everybody knows you can't trust rhythm guitar players. Under that wavin' hair is a guy who wants to score."

Jackie decided that the best way to deal with Tony's silliness was to ignore it. At least it was better than the clenched fists and the threats. Tony was becoming more mature. She almost hated to admit it, but it was so.

"Tony, why are we here?"

"Do you like him?" persisted Tony. "I don't like him, and if I were you, I wouldn't trust him."

"He's just a friend," sighed Jackie. She turned to

the young man waiting patiently in the doorway and called out, "Thanks, Carl."

"Everything all right?" Carl called back.

"Yes. See you Wednesday. Good night."

The door opened and closed and Carl was gone.

"Did you hear how ya said good night?" Tony wanted to know.

"No. How did I say it?"

Tony thought a minute, then shook his head. "I don't wanna get into it, except it didn't have a regular 'good night' sound. You added something to it."

"What are we doing here?" Jackie asked again, tired of the game.

There was a long pause, then Tony said quietly, "I want ya to help me learn Butler's routine."

"You're kidding!" gasped Jackie. But when she looked into Tony's face, she realized at once that he wasn't kidding. He had probably never been so serious about anything in his life.

"I wanna try for the lead in the show. Think I can do it?"

It was a crucial question and it deserved the respect of a serious answer. Jackie's mind raced, considering the needs of the role and Tony's capabilities. Briefly she thought of what might happen with Tony and Laura dancing duets of such high sexuality. But she dismissed those thoughts with the honesty that was characteristic of her. Whatever happened happened. There was nothing she could do to stop it. You can't keep two people apart who want to be together. Tony had worked hard for a chance, and he ought to have it.

"I think so," she told him seriously, her green eyes meeting his blue ones.

Tony smiled down at her. "Wanna help?"

"Sure. Why not?"

"Wanna start now?"

"Sure. Why not?"

They worked hard at it, Jackie dancing Laura's part, while Tony took Butler's. Alone in the vast rehearsal hall with only the taped music and their own images reflected in the wall mirrors, they practiced the romantic *pas de deux* that were the heart and soul of the show. They had seen the routines danced so often that they knew them by heart. But knowing them by heart and making your body respond to the unfamiliar patterns were two very different things. Especially when they had no director to tell them where they were going wrong.

Hesitant at first and then with growing confidence, they danced and danced, their bodies weaving around each other. Now it was Jackie who was dominant, now Tony; now they melded together as though they were one, and you could almost not tell where one of them left off and the other began. Between them there was a sensuality that was what Jesse had had in mind when choreographing this dance. The magnetism that pulled man and woman together and the pressures that pulled them apart.

Maybe it was because they were close that they danced so well together. Each knew the other's body well and how to make it respond, and that mattered.

But it was grueling work. Over and over until morning light broke through the studio windows and the two of them, glistening with sweat, realized with astonishment that they had literally danced the night away.

It was a very tired Tony and Jackie who stepped out into the cold air of a winter morning.

"What do you think?" asked Tony.

Jackie shook her head. "No. It's what do *you* think?"

Tony shrugged. "I don't know," he said honestly. "Think I should try it?"

"You've got the routine down."

"But is it good enough?" Tony's face looked strained. Blue shadows smudged the hollows under his eyes.

"Yes." There was nothing more to say.

"You going home now?" asked Tony. He appeared flustered, which was unnatural for him. "Sure, ya goin' home. Where else would you go at six in the morning?"

"Nowhere. Well, I'll see you in a few hours."

"Yeah," he nodded. "Thanks."

Jackie was heading for the subway on the corner when she heard Tony calling after her. "Hey, Jackie." She turned, waiting for him to catch up.

But he stood there a few feet away from her, not coming any closer, his blue eyes fixed on her face.

"Don't go," he said so softly that she wasn't certain she heard him right.

Slowly with a great effort as though he were bringing every word up from somewhere buried deeply inside him, Tony began to speak. And as he did, he moved closer and closer to Jackie, until they were only inches apart.

"It's like I wanna say somethin', but it's hard, 'cause I never grew up saying nice things, so it's hard for me to do it now. All I know is that I really had somethin' nice with you . . . comfortable, y'know? And . . . and I was wrong actin' like I did. And . . . look, I don't wanna lose you, 'cause you make me feel better when we're together. Like I said before, comfortable. And if I do the same for you, I just think that . . . maybe . . . we should try being together again. I hope you believe me this time, 'cause it's all true."

Tears sprang to Jackie's eyes from the intensity of her emotion. She'd given up hope of ever hearing anything like this from Tony, and she'd wanted to hear it for so long! He needed her! That's what he was saying. He loved her and he needed her and he wanted her back!

Without a word she stepped into Tony's arms, which opened to receive her. Their lips met in a long, deep kiss. And was it Jackie's tears that wet Tony's lashes, or was there some moisture there already?

They treated themselves to a cab, a rickety Checker whose springs had sprung, and which gave them the bumpiest ride of their lives all the way back to Jackie's house.

They were so exhausted by the time they climbed the stairs together that they couldn't keep their eyes open. After all, they'd rehearsed all day with Jesse and all night without him. Falling into the apartment, they shut their eyes for immediate sleep.

Chapter Thirteen

IT STILL WASN'T COMING RIGHT, AND Jesse was at the end of his rope. In his head he had a complete vision of what he wanted, what he knew the show should be. Everybody was pulling hard to make that vision come to life, but it wasn't happening. Between the conception and the execution was a vast area where anything and everything could go wrong. So far they'd actually been pretty lucky. The theater had been given over to the technicians, who were creating a multimedia explosion unprecedented in theatrical history, that is, if they didn't blow the fuses and black out the entire eastern seaboard.

The cast was in the rehearsal hall daily for long practice sessions. Having learned each routine separately and having practiced them all until they were numb, they were now putting them all together and seeing what kind of sense they made. Soon they would be in dress rehearsal, the last milestone before opening night. There would be light rehearsals and sound rehearsals and light and sound rehearsals with and without the dancers. The scenery was terribly complicated, so complicated that it wasn't being built in a shop for assembly later, but directly onto the stage of the theater, so that there would be no unpleasant surprises about what did and didn't fit.

And still it wasn't working for Jesse. He threw new combinations at them; chucked out earlier routines and a day later chucked them back in again. And everybody in the company knew exactly where the trouble lay. With the male lead. With Butler Willson.

Jesse knew he was wrong for the part; by now he had admitted as much to himself. But it was too late to change it; opening night was less than two weeks away; how can you go out and find a new principal dancer who would be able to learn all those complicated routines? Butler was a good dancer, a very skilled dancer. He might not have art, but he did have craft. It's just that the role was wrong for him, or he was wrong for the role, or both. But maybe the audience wouldn't notice. Maybe they'd be so dazzled by the score and the lasers and the pyrotechnics on stage and the complexity of the central ballet and the competence of the dancers that they wouldn't miss the sensuality, the electricity that should be flowing between the leads.

The hell they wouldn't! Jesse Benton didn't put shows on for morons, and he didn't cheat his audiences either. Not when they were paying a fifty dollar top, the cost per good ticket for this show, which thanks to the technical effects was one of the most expensive ever to come to Broadway.

Naturally all of this heartache didn't make Jesse's temper any sweeter. Of all directors dance directors are probably the most temperamental, and Jesse's temperament was among the most explosive, registering seven point two on the Richter scale.

So it was with no welcoming smile that Jesse looked up to see a very nervous Tony Manero approaching him as he sat in his private space working out new combinations to terrorize the company with.

Manero was looking as though he were wanting something, and Jesse was in no mood to give. He'd had his eye on Tony since the beginning; the boy had the makings of a superlative dancer. At first Jesse had expected trouble because Manero stood out so from the others and was so very distinctive in style. Also there had been . . . a little something . . . between him and Laura, and it had seemed to Jesse that Tony was taking it badly.

But things had worked out well. The boy was a hard and willing worker and a quick learner. As for Laura, Jesse knew her well and had seen this kind of thing before with Laura. She was able to take care of herself and was good at snuffing out firmly any residual unpleasantness. Laura was a thoroughgoing professional, and the show always came first with her.

But why was Manero looking at him with such apprehension? Why the hesitant feet? Why the diffident manner? He put down his workbook and waited.

At last Tony spoke.

"I think I can do it."

"Do what?" But even as he said it, Jesse knew exactly what Tony meant, and a surge of excitement coursed through him and brought him up out of his chair. He was remembering the attraction between Laura and Tony and the antagonism. He flashed on how good they looked together. Where Butler's pale looks were completely wiped off the stage by Laura, Tony's vividness could stand up to hers. In his way he was as striking as she was in hers.

"What makes you think you can do it?" demanded Jesse.

"I've tried it." Tony's mouth was so dry he could barely get the words out.

"Show me!" commanded the director, and all Tony could do was nod.

From that moment things happened so fast they were a blur to Tony. Jesse hustled him into the main rehearsal room on the double and conferred with Joy at the side of the hall where they couldn't be overheard. Tony saw Joy's look of startled disbelief change to a speculative expression as she glanced over at Tony. She looked as though she were seeing him for the first time.

Next stop was Laura. Standing against the back wall of the studio, pale with apprehension and a little sick to his stomach, Tony watched Jesse speak to his star. He saw Laura's face redden, her head shake in annoyance, and her entire body express "no" clearly. But Jesse was the boss, and Jesse was insisting, demanding, overruling.

He looked over at Jackie rather desperately, receiving a wide smile of encouragement.

Now Joy was collecting the dancers and shepherding them back from their break.

"We'll go to the first number." Jesse's voice was an automatic silencer, and the dancers sought their positions. Butler got up to join the line, but Jesse waved him off.

"Butler, please sit this one out. Tony!"

The blond couldn't believe his ears. "What do you mean, sit this out?" he fairly shrieked.

"I think you understand," Jesse told him quietly.

The boy's lower lip went into a pout. "No, I don't," he insisted.

"Neither do I," said Laura suddenly.

"Sure you do," snapped Jesse. "Positions. Tony!"

With beads of sweat already forming on his brow, Tony stepped up to Laura and put his hand upon her waist as the first position of the routine called for. He could feel her shrink away under his touch, but suddenly the music came out of the speakers, and the dance began. Instantly Laura became all professionalism and was dancing with Tony as though they'd been rehearsing for weeks.

This was it! This was exactly what Jesse had been looking for. The style, the merging of the two dancers into one entity. This was his private vision made flesh!

He and Joy exchanged glances of pleasure and excitement as they watched Tony and Laura move into the *pas de deux*.

Suddenly Tony made a misstep, and it threw him so out of sync that he forgot his place in the routine. The entire sequence just went out of his head, and he stood there, feeling like a fool.

"Satisfied?" hissed Laura at Jesse, furious.

Scarlet with mortification, Tony could only turn and run. He couldn't bear to stay here another second, and he headed for the exit, tears of anger stinging his eyelids. Jackie took a step toward him but thought better of it and stood miserably watching him go, her heart going with him.

With a smirk, Butler glided up into his place by Laura's side; he felt totally vindicated by Tony's failure.

Tony was going down the steps two at a time when the door above him was flung open and Jesse's voice yelled at him, "Where the hell are you going?"

"I'm leavin'."

"Wait," called Jesse, but Tony didn't listen. He kept on going.

"I said *wait!*" exploded Jesse in a voice accustomed to being obeyed, freezing Tony right in his tracks.

Jesse started down the stairs.

"Whatta ya want?" demanded Tony. He was so ashamed to be seen like this, distraught, a failure, a screwup.

"You don't walk out of here like this and expect to come back," snapped Jesse.

"That right?" The old Manero machismo was asserting itself in rash and useless defiance.

"Yeah, that's right," Jesse told him levelly. "Leave now and you're over."

"What the hell would *you* do?"

The director shook his head. "Don't worry about what I would do. I'm not the one who's on the line. You are."

Tony stuck his chin out stubbornly. "I ain't havin' nobody laughin' at me."

"Who are you? Somebody special?"

"What?!" He didn't have to stand here and take this!

"I said who are you? Somebody special? What did you ever do that means anything? What did you ever do?"

The veins in Tony's arms stood out as his fists clenched angrily. "Who're you talking to?" he yelled.

Jesse took two more steps down. "I'm talking to you," he grated. "What did you ever do? Why, do you think you're so good you're going to score in some other show? Do you?? The only good thing you ever scored was Laura, but you even blew that because you got too heavy." His voice lowered a bit. "You're different animals, and no matter how much you carry on, you can't change that. But if you were half-smart, you'd use it!"

"What are you talking about?" Tony demanded.

Jesse came one step nearer. Now only a single step separated the two men; they could hear each other's breathing, almost hear each other's hearts beating.

"Listen good," said Jesse softly. "Because you're going to hear this only one time. In this business I don't care about you, and you don't have to care about me. All we have to care about is the show. That's it! That's what got you here, and that's what's going to keep you here." He looked sharply at Tony, satisfied that the boy was listening with every bit of his attention.

"If you can't follow that, follow this. If you want to dance here, you follow *my* rules. This is not a democracy! You are my responsibility, and that's real bad news for anybody who doesn't want to work. Because I'm going to keep pushing until you think you're going to die. But whoever makes it through will be the best dancers in this city! You're not the greatest dancer ever to hit the boards, but you have a raw anger and presence, and that's what I need. So don't think I'm standing here because I want you to be my friend, because I don't. I'm standing here because I think you got the moves and the attitude to help me make this show work. So where are you going? Back to cleaning tables." Jesse shook his head in disgust. "Go on. I've wasted enough time already." Turning, he walked quickly up the stairs.

Tony stood watching him for only a minute, then he walked down the stairs, heading for the real world, away from the make-believe and the sweat and the aching muscles and the sore feet and the arrogant directors who can feed you any line of tyrannical crap because they think they own you.

"First positions," called Joy again.

Jackie couldn't believe that Tony had really gone. Was this it? The end of all their hopes, their weary hours of practicing, the end of Tony's ambitions.

Laura took a step forward. "What happened?" she asked, unable to contain her curiosity.

"Aren't you here to dance?" snapped Jesse.

There was an uneasy rustle and murmur in the company. Bad vibes when the star and the director have nasty words in public. Bad luck too.

Joy reached for the cassette button, but before her finger could hit it, the rehearsal hall door swung open with a bang, and Tony Manero strode into the room, his head held high. He walked directly up to Butler, who was standing next to Laura, waiting to dance.

The two dancers locked eyes, while everybody waited without breathing for the outcome.

"Butler," said Jesse softly. It was all he had to say.

"No! This is real bull!" wailed Butler, heading for the door. "Just wait until I call my agent!"

Jesse gave a nod of his head to Joy, and she hit the cassette button. The music poured into the room, and the dancers began moving.

It was flawless, one of those pure moments that time allows so few of us so rarely, when the tip of the human finger brushes against the stars. With one fluid movement Laura and Tony swept into the dance, their bodies in perfect coordination, their understanding of each other and of the steps so complete that there was no angle from which they were not perfection. Drawn into the magic of the two of them, the rest of the company found new insight, and for the first time they all moved as an ensemble, as a silken unit of rhythm and grace rather than a collection of individual dancers.

Jesse Benton caught his breath and blinked the stinging tears back. This was dearer than his dearest hope. This was what he wanted the world to see. This was how he hoped to be remembered. As the creator of all this beauty, of poetry in motion.

Chapter Fourteen

THERE WERE TIMES IN THE WEEKS THAT followed when Tony honestly believed he wouldn't survive. He had sudden chilling visions of perishing from exhaustion on the day of opening night, and that wimp Butler Willson, called back from a Bahamas vacation, bleached by the sun and rested, would go on in his place and take all the bows. And you know what? When the visions passed, Tony was too tired to care. Death would be a welcome relief from this endless torture.

Now Tony realized why actors sometimes go mad and strangle directors. Shooting was too clean, too distant. What you really wanted was to do it with your own hands; stabbing was second best, because you would wade in the gore. If there was any man in the world he could call his enemy, Tony knew it was Jesse Benton.

"Again! From the top! Positions! Again! Again! Tony, you can do better than that. Tony, I don't like your extension. Again! Do it again!" He heard Jesse's voice in his sleep, what little sleep he was able to snatch, and the dream voice made his aching muscles twitch in blind obedience. The rehearsal hall became Nazi Germany with music. "Again! Again! Again!"

One of the things he found most difficult in his elevation to principal dancer was the interpretation of the *acting* of the role. *Inferno* was a most complex work of art, but Tony as a chorus dancer had given its subtleties very little thought. Now that he was playing the male lead, the interpretation of the complexities was his responsibility, and he was still feeling his way into the role.

Basically what Jesse had crammed into one show was just about every manifestation of the human condition. Life and death, Heaven and Hell, good and evil, love and hate, earthiness and spirituality, chastity and sin—every polarity was examined in the dance. The single thread of the plot, inspired by Dante, was the human soul in search of immortality. In case that sounds highfalutin, intellectual and dull, be assured that the soul in its odyssey comes into contact and conflict with many temptations, most of them in the form of lightly clad and very beautiful women. So the tired businessman, that legendary patron of the theater, would hardly go away disappointed.

Tony played an Everyman, and Laura portrayed all the female parts—the romantic chaste love, the temptress, the demon who tries to drag him down to Hell and at the great climax of the play, the sanctified Beatrice type who ascends with Tony to Heaven. If you added to the thread of the plot the most advanced visual effects that lasers and computer chips had ever brought to the theater, the most dazzling and revealing costumes, the most beautiful dancers, choreography so erotic the stage sizzled and an explosive rock and roll score, you had a sort of pale description of what Jesse was trying to do.

What he hoped to achieve was to knock his audiences right out of their seats, kick them around the aisles, mop up the floors with them and send them home to mother shaking and crying and secure in the knowledge that they'd never seen anything like this before and never would again. In short, he wanted to give them their money's worth. The costs on this show were so high coming in that his reputation was riding on the sale of every ticket. His entire life was knotted up in this production; is it any wonder that he turned into a tyrant?

Inferno had already outstripped *Cats* as the show most talked about, most written about in advance. Nobody knew what the plot was; that was a bigger secret than missile base sites. Jesse was adamant about not revealing anything of the story line in advance; nor would he describe any of the spectacular visual effects. He wanted no preconceptions or misconceptions, no oversell or ballyhoo. *Inferno* would be revealed on opening night and not before. No previews. Speculation was rampant. Liz Smith reported that a live volcano would erupt on stage, covering the first six rows of spectators in lava.

On the days that the technical and dress rehearsals were scheduled, Jesse hired a security police force of three men to patrol the theater armed and make certain that nobody unauthorized had penetrated the locked building. Nor was he unaware of the publicity value of the Pinkertons; it only made the columnists try harder. Somebody from the *New York Post–Examiner* was caught trying to bribe a sound engineer for information, using as a come-on a season pass to the Knicks games. The engineer, a Lakers fan, turned the snoop in.

Scheduled to open in late January, the show was already sold out through August.

Tony knew nothing of any of this. He was living in a vacuum. Get up. Go to rehearsal. Work all day. Bandage feet. Come home. Try to eat. Fall down on bed fully dressed. Twitch instead of sleep. Get up. Go to rehearsal. Thank God for Jackie, who fed him soups and rubbed his back and shoulders and the tension knot at the base of his neck.

All the elements of the show—sets, costumes, choreography, were coming together now in long runthroughs with and without special effects. These runthroughs would start at ten in the morning and go on as late as seven or eight in the evening. In addition Tony and Laura were put through endless rehearsals of their numbers by Jesse, who drilled them into perfection, or that is, his own idea of perfection, which made perfection itself look tacky.

Granted, these were long and complicated numbers, and they ran a total emotional gamut from spiritual love to dancing sexy. The last act was especially difficult and demanding. This was where Tony had to battle off all the forces of Hell in order to attain Heaven.

"Heaven" was the biggest secret of all; it was a giant white disc that appeared to be built into the floor but was actually a hydraulic platform that moved up and up without any visible means of locomotion. The disc appeared to be suspended in space . . . ascending to heaven with Tony and Laura as a modern day Dante and Beatrice wrapped in each other's arms, poised on the platform. If that didn't bring the final curtain down on a cheering semihysterical elite group of first-nighters, then McDonald's doesn't sell hamburgers.

The dance that preceded the ascent was the most challenging of all, as the lovers find each other after searching through two other acts. Tony and Laura would appear at opposite ends of the stage and in a spectacular series of leaps would reach each other, entwine, dance a climactic routine heavy with emotion, and in the end go up to Heaven. The leaps had to match with perfect symmetry, each leap of each dancer the identical length as the previous one, and required split-second timing. But when you saw it from the orchestra, you could never forget it as long as you lived.

Funny. It wasn't long ago that Tony was driven by two ambitions. To dance on Broadway and to dance with Laura. And now he was achieving both his dreams and he was too damn pooped to enjoy it.

Still, in the moments when his energy burned high, he did realize how great a dancer Laura Ravell was, and how perfectly they matched as a dancing team. Each struck sparks from the other; they were like two sides of the same coin. The yin and the yang, masculine and feminine principles of life. On the stage she was the unattainable and infinitely desirable epitome of woman.

Off the stage Tony wanted no part of her. He had the woman he wanted, the woman who was right for him, who made him happy. And he was secure enough to turn his back on Laura no matter how tempting she appeared.

And she *was* trying to tempt him. At first he thought it might be his imagination, even his old ego acting up. Maybe it was nothing more than residual heat from the routines taking its time cooling off. But he wasn't imagining things. Every time he looked up, Laura was watching him with that look on her face that spelled trouble. That come-here-Tony-I-want-you look; nobody in the world could do it like she could. It was a look he had to turn away from, and turn away he did, time after time. He never let her corner him alone; and he was constantly on his guard against her.

Laura knew that Tony was living with Jackie; it was no secret. Everyone had accepted their relationship, everyone but Laura. If anything it made her hotter for Tony. Even as a child she would rather take another kid's toy away than play with the many she already had.

The problem was that Tony didn't trust her. He knew that underneath the smolder was an ice-hard personality with a vindictive streak a mile wide. Tony had been raised in the streets of Brooklyn, and he had plenty of smarts. With all her class and all her style, Laura was a gutter fighter. Tony recognized one when he saw one; he used to be one himself.

His vibes told him that if Laura couldn't get her mitts on him, she'd try to mess him up in some important way, and his vibes were never wrong.

Besides, Tony hated unfinished business, and Laura Ravell came under that heading. There were still things he wanted to get straight between them, once and for all time.

Then one day everything stopped. Rehearsals were over. It was only a day or two before opening night, and it was time for a rest. No more work.

There's an old joke about a guy who lives next door to a boiler factory. All his life long, noise, noise, noise. All day, noise. All night, noise. One night the boiler factory breaks down, and suddenly there is complete, total, sweet blessed silence. And the guy sits bolt upright in bed and screams, "What the hell was that?"

That's how Tony felt. His body protested. His mind protested. He couldn't rest; he couldn't believe there were no more long, agonizing rehearsals and run-throughs. And he suddenly felt unprepared and very vulnerable. Maybe if he had another week . . .

He and Jackie walked over to the theater and looked at the marquee and their names on the posters. It didn't seem real.

"Can you believe it's really going to happen?" asked Jackie, thrilled. Then when Tony didn't answer, she pressed him. "Aren't you excited?"

"Yeah," said Tony, subdued. He appeared lost in thought.

"What's wrong?"

He wasn't sure how to tell her.

"What's wrong?" she asked him again, anxious now.

Tony squared his shoulders. "Look, Jackie. Listen.

I gotta go somewhere. I'll see ya later at your place, all right? Are you okay, or would ya like me to walk ya back home?"

"I'm okay. Where are you going?"

"Where?" echoed Tony.

"Yes, where?"

He drew a deep breath. "I've got to talk to her," he said.

Jackie felt a sudden chill on her backbone. "Laura?"

"I know what you're thinkin', but it's not that. There's just something I gotta say."

Biting her lip to keep the tears back, Jackie cried, "Why? It's going to start all over again."

But Tony was shaking his head. "It won't."

"How do you know it won't?"

Tony looked her right in the eye. " 'Cause I can't handle any more guilt," he told her plainly.

She stared at him for a moment, then burst into a great shout of laughter. Bending down, Tony scooped her small body up in his arms and gave her an enormous hug. Then he went off to do what he had to do.

When Laura opened her apartment door to him, she stared at Tony, her amber eyes unfathomable. "Yes?" she asked as though she'd never seen him before.

"I got to ask ya something."

"What is it? Rehearsals are over." She still stood in the doorway.

"Can I come in?"

Slowly she stood out of his path, letting him into her marble-floored foyer with its sculptured dancers on marble and lucite pedestals. She was, as he'd expected, very beautiful, dressed in perfectly cut skintight pants of black leather topped by a cowlneck cashmere sweater in the exact shade of her eyes. Yet all her beauty made an impression only on his eyes, not on his heart.

"Y'know, we've been working pretty hard on this show," Tony began.

"Yes?" She certainly wasn't going to make it easy.

"An' I don't want any bad feelings we might have to hurt the show."

"Tony, I don't have any bad feelings toward you. You just have this need to control people."

"Control?" He had no idea what she was talking about.

"Exactly. You just want people to do what you want them to do."

Tony scowled; his dark brows contracted and shadowed his eyes. "You still don't know what I'm about."

"I think I do." She surveyed him coolly as though pricing him for market.

Tony stiffened, and his jaw tightened. "Look, I don't wanna fight about it. I just wanna know that you won't start act'n up out there."

Laura's nostrils flared in anger. " 'Acting up'?" she repeated. "I'm a professional! Why don't you run along now?"

He still hadn't gotten through to her. Now she had him totally confused. "Y'know, I don't know why I have to feel like this."

"Like what?"

"Like I gotta prove myself."

"Who's asking you to?" challenged Laura.

Tony put his hands up in surrender. "Nobody, that's what's getting me crazy. Why do I have to prove myself to you? Did you ever prove yourself to me?"

Laura tilted her chin up at him and narrowed her eyes. "Prove what? I don't have to prove anything. You didn't come here because of the show. You came here to tell me that you think you're just as good as I am, didn't you?"

"I don't think that." Tony shook his head.

"Yes, you do!" Laura's voice went up a notch in volume. "And to answer your question, you're not!

But you've figured a way to work around that detail, didn't you?"

"What're you saying?" demanded Tony.

"I'm saying that since the day we met all you were interested in was what doors I could open for you! You've never cared for a damn thing in your life except your own needs! *Everyone* has needs, not just you!"

Stung, Tony looked around the apartment. "You don't look so needy to me!" he threw at her.

"You smug creep, do you think that a room full of junk fulfills real needs? When will you finally wake up?"

Unable to hold onto his temper a second longer, Tony flared right back at her. "No! When are *you* gonna wake up? When are you gonna stop thinking that everybody always wants to use you?"

"You more than anyone!" She was shouting now, and a vein was throbbing in her forehead.

"Don't say that!"

"I'll say what I want!" she snarled. "You're like a duplication of evey pathetically ambitious dancer I've ever met!" Laura was out of control now, or she wouldn't have permitted herself to say what she said next.

"Why did you go back with her?" And her voice held unshed tears.

"I wanted to! I trust her!"

"Didn't you ever mean anything you said?"

"I meant everything!" cried Tony. "You just never believed it."

They stood glaring at each other like two panting animals, each blaming the other for the failure that belonged to both of them.

"What about now?" asked Laura softly. "How do you feel now? The way we dance together, I know you must feel something."

"I do," admitted Tony.

"What? What do you feel?" She raised her beautiful eyes to his and they were glowing.

"I respected you more than anything," said Tony quietly, sadly.

"If you really mean it, you wouldn't just let it go." She moved closer to him. They were so close now they almost touched.

"And I thought we had something good," he said huskily.

"We do." Her voice was almost a whisper, and her lips, so firm and moist, were only inches away.

Tony pulled his eyes away from hers. "But now I have something better."

She recoiled from him like a wounded snake, angry and bitter. "Do you?"

He nodded. He did. He really did. This proved it. It was as though he'd set himself a test and passed it.

"You came here wondering about the show," said Laura crisply. "Don't worry. I'll carry you and no one will know that you really don't have it. Give her my best."

She opened the door pointedly and held it open. Tony nodded and turned to go. But he turned back again to look at Laura, beautiful, talented, neurotic Laura.

"Ya know the real trouble here," he told her quietly. "We were never lovers. We were competition."

And suddenly time compressed, squeezed shut like a concertina, and it was opening night. Magic time, panic time, dancers being sick in the ladies' room time.

Jesse was everywhere, in the giant sound booth at the front of the mezzanine, sitting in front of the console, giving orders through the headset to the stage manager below, who also wore a headset so that he could give orders to everybody else. There had been a last-minute sound check, light check, video check, laser check; incredibly, everything was working.

After the mechanics, the dancers had to be seen to. Tony was of course Jesse's top priority; this was not only his first leading role, it was his first job of any kind, Broadway or off-Broadway.

"How are you feeling?" asked Jesse, sticking his head into Tony's dressing room.

The boy nodded, too tense to utter a word. He was sitting in his costume, leg warmers on over his tights, his legs stretched out in front of him. Although the dressing room was a little on the chilly side, Tony's forehead was already gleaming with sweat, and he was looking a little green.

"I only want to tell you one thing. When you stand in front of that audience, remember you're not one of them. But dance for them, dance for yourself."

Tony forced a weak little smile. "Think they'd mind if I called it off?"

Jesse smiled and gave Tony's shoulder an encouraging pat. "They might. They just might."

Chapter Fifteen

THERE IS NO HUSH OF EXPECTANCY QUITE like the one that falls over a first-night audience that smells a hit show. Maybe the hush on the first morning of the first day of the world was something like it, but much less exciting. After all, it took God only six days to create the world, but it took Jesse Benton more than six months to create *Inferno*. And God didn't have lasers.

The house lights dimmed, and the conductor raised his baton, and between that moment and the one in which the overture began, a silence so profound as to be palpable fell over the audience. Not one cough, not one rustle of a program or a candy wrapper. The audience was already in awe. Mostly of itself, for being the few thousand elite to be present on the evening of the creation. Too bad God didn't have an audience; maybe then He wouldn't have invented cockroaches.

Swifty and silently the chorus dancers took their places on the stage, assuming the positions in which they'd be found when the curtain went up. Jackie gave Tony one last kiss for good luck; he seemed too dazed to notice.

I can't do it. I'll never make it through. I don't want to be a dancer. Who the hell ever said I had to be a dancer? I'm sick. They'll have to let me go home. I don't feel too good.

Tony was absolutely panic-stricken, what theater people call "opening-night jitters." His feet wouldn't obey him. He'd forgotten all the routines; he couldn't even remember the first step he was supposed to dance. The overture was half-over, in three minutes he'd be making his first entrance, and he couldn't remember whether he started out on his left foot or his right. *Feets, don't fail me now.*

The curtain was up now, revealing a surrealistic landscape lit beautifully and subtly. The chorus had begun to move sinuously, their narrow bodies sketching the story, just as the chorus in the ancient Greek tragedies dedicated to the gods danced out the story.

And it was time for Tony's entrance, and suddenly it was all right. He took his first leap out onto the stage, heard the applause, ignored it and went on dancing. His body remembered perfectly every movement, each nuance. He danced with confidence, his body showing to advantage in the cleverly made ragged costume with hidden bits of mirror that sent the light back in splintered scintillations.

And Laura was dancing with him now, the woman he was to lose, to seek, to find only at the end, when he brought her to Heaven. They danced slowly, romantically, spiritually, with no hint of eroticism; that would come later, when the audience least expected it. When they finished their first *pas de deux,* the audience went wild, refusing to allow the dancing to continue until Laura and Tony had taken individual bows. If they only knew what was in store for them. . . .

In the sound booth, his eyes glued to the stage, Jesse Benton exulted. It was going better than he'd hoped. He was going to have a hit on his hands; he could tell that from the audience reaction already. And this was only the mild stuff.

The story unfolded, and the dancing became more and more erotic as the soul proceeded on its earthly odyssey. Gasps of delight mingled with shock and surprise and even a little horror sent tremors over the audience. Tony's athletic body, Laura's slim one met, joined, twined, parted, met again.

When the curtain dropped on the first act, the applause was a crashing of sound waves beating against the stage. Then the audience raced up the aisles to the lobbies to light cigarettes, see and be seen and find out what everybody else thought of the show.

Jesse left the sound booth to eavesdrop. He caught a gratifying number of "fabulouss" and "incredibles" and not too many "disgustings" to discourage him.

And he was saving his heaviest guns for the second half. Here was where most of the surprises were. The descent into the Underworld scene, the lighting effects. And best of all, the ascent. Here is where he had concentrated the most spectacular of the dances, each one more outrageous than the one before, so that the show built and built without a letdown.

Backstage the dancers were cooling down, rubbing sore muscles, crouching and stretching, making costume changes and grabbing as much rest as they could. This was the only part of the evening they were able to rest, this twenty minute intermission between the acts.

Having made his costume change and checked his makeup, Tony was toweling his hair dry in his dressing room. Exhilaration ran through his veins like fireworks, giving out little pops of energy. He was on a high, a rush that came from sheerest physical and mental exertion. This was the most exciting evening of his life; he had totally lost his jitters and was impatiently waiting for the second act. He intended to knock them all dead, because this was where he did his most spectacular dancing.

Once more it was time. The audience were returning to their seats and the lights were flickering to signal the start of the second act. Tony stood up and took off his bathrobe. He had to be on stage before the curtain went up.

In the sound booth Jesse was relaying last-minute instructions to the stage manager, who was passing them along as cues to the technical crew. Everybody was tense, because this was the half of the show that would make or break them.

The curtain rose, revealing Tony in a single spotlight. Around him the terrain was as yet unrecognizable, and the music was a lonely wail.

And NOW! Now it happened! Lights went on everywhere reflecting off mirrors to bounce around the stage like crazy billiard balls. The lasers flashed on and off with the power of miniature suns. An eerie fog rose from the floor of the stage, and through the fog half-naked bodies could be seen crawling and writhing. These were the damned, the lost souls, and Tony was in Hell!

To the sides of the stage, steel high-tech cages held even more damned souls. These were the singers, who were not expected to writhe.

Upstage was the set, the Gates of Hell, a giant pair of jaws with huge fangs for teeth. The effect, bursting on the audience all at once, was so spectacular it brought cheers. The people sitting in the back rows stood up to see the set better.

Now the damned had seen Tony and were crawling toward him, reaching up to drag him down, to make him one of them. He danced back, away from them, eluding them, but they followed, clawing at his legs, his clothing, stretching their etiolated arms up to him.

Now some of the damned were rising up out of the dense mist, and the audience gasped again. The dancers were beautiful women, and their breasts were bare! They wore little more than dancers' G-strings; these represented the sexual temptations of Hell.

Tony danced with one of them, then with another, as

they attempted to seduce him and damn him forever. These were highly sexual routines, and Jesse had assigned the most important of the female parts to Jackie, understanding that she and Tony were lovers, knowing that the fact of it would make the dance more exciting and convincing.

But try though they might, the lost women could gain no power over Tony; his stainless purity defeated them all.

Now it was the turn of stronger demons. A half dozen of the male dancers dressed in skintight jumpsuits and eerie masks took the center of the stage armed with ropes. Since the sexual demons couldn't capture Tony, they would see what brute strength powered by evil could accomplish. With their ropes they would bind Tony and carry him down to the deepest part of Hell, from which there was no escape. They danced nearer and nearer to Tony, taunting him with their ropes, strutting and prancing to flaunt their power.

But he fought them all, his muscular body darting here and there like summer lightning, evading them, striking a blow here or a kick there. Still, they were six to one, and their strength came from Satan himself; would they not eventually overpower him? Was it not inevitable?

No, an invisible shield seemed to protect Tony, a cloak fashioned of the power of God that gave him the strength of ten, and he danced on, now faltering a little, yet always regaining his magical prowess.

Then the music reached a bizarre crescendo, and the Gates of Hell began to yawn open. The wicked fangs drew apart slowly, until there between them an evilly beautiful creature appeared—Laura, as the most powerful of Satan's minions.

Laura was dressed in a high-leg red leotard and high-heeled dancing sandals. Both her arms were held high over her head, and in her clenched hands was a whip, symbol of her evil authority. She was breathtaking. If she could not gain dominion over Tony's soul, what power could?

He was trapped. Downstage were the male demons with their ropes, and upstage stood Laura, Her Satanic Majesty. It seemed hopeless. But with one quick movement of his strong arm, Tony had ripped the whip out of Laura's hands and was using it to slash at the demons, to drive them back, to destroy evil with a weapon of evil.

Now it was only Tony and Laura who were antagonists. And she was the most powerful foe of all, using her diabolical beauty to destroy. It was Tony's immortal soul that was at stake here, and she had all the experience of the tens of thousands of years that she'd spent at this very endeavor, the capturing of a soul. All Tony had was the protection of his innocence and his faith.

What Jesse Benton had created here was possibly the most sensual ballet ever seen, a choreography that left almost nothing to the imagination. The stage belonged to the two of them, and it was as though they were in a private bower with a bed draped in black velvet and only blood-colored candles for light.

Laura's beauty was never so unreal as it was now. Her body was a fluid column of fire, her hair alive and glowing. Her powerful long legs in their mesh stockings curved around Tony's body, pulling him so closely into her that it seemed as though he were possessing her and she him. Because they had been to bed together, their bodies were imprinted on each other, and this choreography was in the marrow of their bones.

He was weakening now; she was tearing at the fabric of his innocence, destroying his protective cloak of goodness. What flesh could resist the most beautiful woman ever created? He told himself that she had been created by Satan, not God, and that his immortal soul was the most prized thing between Heaven and earth, but what was the value of a soul when the flesh was so beautiful and so beckoning?

He danced away from her time after time, only to dance back, drawn by her allure. He dominated her, pulling her by her hair, bending her over deeply, grasping her tightly, but his domination was always of short duration. Laura's power was stronger than his . . . she had him firmly in her grasp, he bent to kiss her lips as the price of his soul. The drums got louder, more rhythmic, a pulse beating like the blood in their veins. And then . . .

Laura's nails raked out and tore open Tony's cheek, dangerously close to the eye. The blood welled up immediately.

Among the dancers, a gasp, and Jackie began to rise, only to be pulled back down again by her partner.

In the sound booth Jesse saw Laura inflict the wound, and he rose with a loud "Damn!" and tore out of the booth and down the side aisle to backstage.

The dance number being over, the audience had noticed nothing. Those in the front rows assumed that the blood was makeup and that it was all in the script. The dancers took their bows to a roar of applause and ran offstage.

"How was it!" Tony was grinning, almost unaware of the injury to his face. He wouldn't even feel the painful throbbing until later, so euphoric was he. Sweat dripped from his body, and his dresser ran over with a towel. Laura took several deep breaths from the portable oxygen machine.

"How's your eye?" cried Jackie.

"Don't worry about it, I'm fine."

Now Jesse exploded backstage like a dark thundercloud.

"What happened? What the hell are you two doing?" he roared.

Tony took a hit off the oxygen mask. "Earnin' a livin'."

Backstage the dancers who were not needed at once were limbering up, shaking their muscles with their hands, bending over to drop their arms loosely to the floor.

Dressers were working on the costume changes, ripping off the soiled clothes and throwing them wordlessly on a big sheet to be bundled up for the laundry cart. Other dressers clapped the new costumes on, knelt at the feet of the dancers to adjust their shoes.

Jesse yanked Tony roughly to one side. "Out there you two are just dancers. You wanna fight, do it on your own time. The show is the thing, not you, the show! When the hell are you gonna learn that?"

This was somewhat unfair to Tony, who hadn't exactly been begging Laura to scratch his face. But he agreed with Jesse wholeheartedly. The show *was* the thing! This was what he'd been waiting to do all his life. And it was better than he'd ever dreamed it could be. With another hit off the oxygen to get his head together and replenish the oxygen he'd used up dancing, Tony was back on the stage, to a fresh crescendo of applause.

Now it was one pyrotechnical sensation after another as the stage manager called the complicated cues to the tech staff. The laser effects were fantastic—a battle in outer space. The music swelled, and the dancers worked their hardest. The audience was beside itself. Nothing had prepared them for this cascade of wonders, this barrage of visual and musical delights. It was a kaleidoscope of colors and shapes, and they hardly knew where to look first.

In one of the brief costume changes, Laura approached Tony. "Tony, after working with you, I have to tell you something I honestly feel." He waited for the compliment. "You don't have it. You don't have it."

Jesse, sitting up in his booth like a commanding general surveying his troops, checked his watch.

"Five minutes more," he told the sound crew. The show only had a little while longer to run, and it was five minutes to takeoff for the ascent.

The music was strong and lyrical now with an overpowering melodic theme, the theme of search that had run through the show.

In opposite wings, Tony and Laura stood poised. This was the number that they had rehearsed so exhaustively. They would come running toward each other taking identical leaps, meet in the exact center of the stage, dance together with the rapture of love found again and take off for Heaven on the great white disc, while the audience came unglued.

The music was building. The dancers came toward each other, twin arrows of grace and light. They came closer and closer to center stage and . . . at the moment of contact . . .

Instead of joining Laura, Tony danced right past her, spinning and dipping, moving like a warrior, a chieftain, while Laura stood transfixed in the middle of the stage, her face white.

Abandoned. He had abandoned her, leaving her to her own devices, while he danced.

And Tony Manero danced. How he danced! His body was here, there, brilliant in its leaps and its struts. And not one step of it rehearsed, not one step of it choreographed. He was improvising the entire thing.

"What the hell is he doing?" yelled Jesse, his eyes wide with panic.

"A solo," remarked the sound man dryly.

And what a solo! "You're afraid to show them how you can dance," Jackie had told him once. "You hold back, afraid to show what you've got." Afraid, was he? He'd show them afraid!

"You don't have it," Pansy Paul the choreographer had told him. "You don't have it," Freddie the bartender had told him. "You don't have it," Laura the world-class ballbuster had told him. *Who* didn't have it? Not Tony Manero. He had it. And he danced to show them who had it.

He danced Bay Ridge and the boys on the block he played stickball with. He danced his First Communion in his white suit with matching Bible. He danced his days as king of the disco. He danced the hard times in New York, down and out with nobody wanting him. He danced Jackie and his feeling for her, a tender, nurturing thing that was still growing. He danced tall, his new pride in himself, in his personhood rather than in his machismo. He danced his self-respect, his new maturity and the honesty of his feelings. All that was inside Tony Manero, and all that came out as he danced.

And now it was time for the ascent, and Tony was dancing on the disc. As the music drew to a shattering climax, the great white platform began to rise. Shafts of searing white light came shooting off its base. Like a spacecraft slowly ascending, the disc with Tony on it moved majestically toward the ceiling of the theater.

Tony looked down. On stage he could see Jackie, looking up at him with love shining from her eyes. In the center of the fifth row center, he could see his mother, her mouth open in astonishment, amazed. He could hear the audience, hysterical, stamping their feet, cheering and whistling. It was pandemonium down there. Theatrical history had been written tonight.

Of course he couldn't hear Jesse, cursing him out like a marine drill sergeant and then deciding to keep Tony's solo in every night from now on. And he couldn't hear Jackie calling, "I love you, Tony Manero," a most unprofessional thing to do, but forgivable this once. And he didn't yet know that in these three short hours he had become one of the most luminous stars on the Broadway stage, and that was just the beginning.

Now all he could see was Laura, staring up at him with those great stricken eyes. Laura, who should have been up here with him according to the script. Laura, overthrown, broken in spirit and left behind.

Inside Tony, the gentleman struggled and broke out. "Laura," he yelled. "Come on, Laura!" The platform wasn't too high off the stage yet; she could still make it. But she'd have to run like hell. He knelt down at the edge of the disc and held his hand out to her. But she stood frozen, unable to take it.

"Come *on!* Laura! You can do it! Hurry!"

She began to move, then broke into a run. As the disc rose higher into the air, she ran faster, reaching the edge almost too late. But Tony grabbed for her hand and held it fast. She took a mighty leap with her long dancer's legs, and he pulled and brought her safely aboard. Together they went up to Heaven, while rockets went off and the lasers created miraculous colors and shapes never seen before.

The audience got its money's worth.

Later when the curtain was down, and bedlam reigned backstage, Tony would slip away. Although tonight was his greatest triumph so far, oddly he didn't feel like sharing it with anybody. Not even Jackie, although he did tell her that none of it would have been possible without her. Not even with Laura, who was giving him the shy smiles of a tamed shrew. Not with the cast or the director. He didn't feel like taking his bows at Sardi's. He didn't want to read the first reviews, which were triumphant. All of that would come later. There was time for everything later. Time was no longer the enemy snapping at his heels. He'd tamed it, domesticated it into something he could wear on his wrist.

No. He didn't really want to be with anybody or do the conventional things.

But what did he want to do? pleaded Jackie.

Funny about that. What Tony Manero really wanted to do was go across the bridge to Bay Ridge and go out struttin'.